all the best from

ENCORE FORSYTH

Gavin MacDonald

ISBN 978 - 1 – 326 – 58170 - 1

Detective Chief Inspector Ian Forsyth Books

Death is my Mistress
The Crime Committee
My Frail Blood
Publish and be Dead
Swallow Them Up
Dishing The Dirt
A Family Affair
Playing Away
Bloody and Invisible Hand
The Truth in Masquerade
I Spy, I Die
A Bow at a Venture
Passport to Perdition
The Plaintive Numbers
The Root of all Evil
Pay Any Price
Murder at he Museum
Murder of an Unknown
The Long Arm
The Forsyth Saga
The Second Forsyth Saga
A Further Forsyth Saga
Double Jeopardy
Rendezvous with Death
A Forsyth Duo
The Man Who Died Twice
Forsyth Triumphant

Science Fiction:
Mysteries of Space and Time

Science Mystery
Amorphous

This volume contains two of the cases brilliantly solved by DCI Ian Forsyth

MURDERS OF NOTE

and

THE ISLAND OF DEATH

FOREWORD

This volume, the twenty-eighth that I have written about my time in the Lothian and Borders Police, contains accounts of two of DCI Ian Forsyth's cases. The first, *Murders of Note,* took place in the August of 1982; the second, *The Island of Death,* in 1995, long after Forsyth had retired from the service and was not supposed to be involved in murder cases any more. I am the person who is most qualified to record all of Forsyth's triumphs because I was his sergeant for most of the time that he was at the height of his fame.

Stories are told, even now, by grizzled veterans at Fettes to new recruits, of the flashes of brilliance that allowed Forsyth to solve cases that had the rest of us totally baffled. Unfortunately, with time, additions have been made to the tales that convince the recruit that these are stories on a par with the accounts of the deeds of Robin Hood or King Arthur and they are loathe to believe that Forsyth ever existed.

I can assure you that he existed all right. I had to cope with him for more years than I care to remember. He was not the easiest of people to work for. He was no good at tasks that had no intellectual challenge and therefore left all the routine work to his underlings. But, if that was something that we at times resented, we had to admit that we also shared in his triumphs when he had solved one of the big ones. And no-one ever asked to be moved from his squad.

I got a great deal of pleasure from revisiting these stirring times. I hope that you get as much pleasure from reading about them.

Alistair MacRae,
Edinburgh, 2016

MURDERS OF NOTE

CHAPTER 1

The Forsyth team was on call that evening, so I ate a frugal dinner, washed down with a non-alcoholic drink and then returned to the Lothian and Borders Police headquarters at Fettes to get on with some paperwork. There was no point in doing anything that required concentration because one was likely to be pulled out in the middle of it and completely lose the thread of what one was doing. I was immersed in the paperwork, and thoroughly bored, when the telephone rang. It was Sergeant Anderson from the front desk.

"Alistair," he said. "I need your help. I have a mugging that needs to be looked at."

"A mugging seems a little down-market for one of the force's best detectives," I suggested to him haughtily.

"I know that," he said plaintively. "But every villain in Edinburgh seems to have decided to go on the rampage tonight. Every officer that I have at my command is already out and about investigating one of those heinous crimes. You are the last shot in my armoury."

"Under these circumstances, how can I refuse to help you out?" I stated. "And I admit that I shall be glad to get as far away as possible from this horrible paperwork."

"So I am doing you a favour?"

"Don't push it," I said. "Just tell me about the mugging."

"A student called Peter Carson was having a drink or two in Casey's Bar in Rose Street. When he left, he was mugged and robbed of money and a watch. Someone found him unconscious and called an ambulance."

"Right," I said, "I will make a report on the incident."

I found out which of the crews it was who had picked up Carson and discovered that they were still at the Infirmary. So I went there and found them awaiting a call. The crew consisted of a burly man called Morrison and a rather slight female called Wentworth.

"Carson had left Casey's Bar and gone up the nearest lane running to George Street when someone came up behind him and clobbered him," Morrison told me. "When we got there, there was the bloke that had found him still looking after him. But, once we arrived, the other bloke sloped off."

“Should I be suspicious about his rapid disappearance?” I asked.

“Happens all the time,” replied Wentworth. “People are quite prepared to help someone who has been mugged, but they don't want the hassle of giving statements to the police and maybe having to appear in court. So they whip off rapidly after we get to the scene.”

“So you brought him here.”

“It's always as well to keep someone who has been bashed on the head in for observation,” Morrison pointed out. “Head wounds can be tricky.”

“And you have no further wisdom or suggestions to offer me?”

“None at all.”

“Thanks for your help anyway.”

I was allowed a few minutes with Carson. Not that it did me much good. He had had a couple of drinks in the Bar and had then left. Since his attacker had been hiding in an alcove, had stepped out once Carson was past and had hit him from behind, he had no idea who had mugged him. He had lost a ten pound note and a five pound note and had had his watch taken. The watch he had bought for a fiver at a stall in the market, so it was not worth anything. He had no memory of anyone acting suspiciously in the bar and was no help whatsoever.

I then paid a visit to Casey's Bar. It was no longer run by an Irishman called Casey but by an Irishman called Desmond Murphy. The owner worked the bar while his wife attended to the food in the kitchen. The three children spent most of their time as waiters but were prepared to turn their hands to whatever was needed. I occupied a stool at the bar counter, showed my warrant card to Murphy and accepted a half pint of beer.

“Had you heard that one of your customers was mugged tonight?” I asked.

“Aye” he said. “Young Carson. The news had filtered through.”

“So you know him.”

“I make a point of getting to know my customers. If they feel wanted, they come back, He's a student doing engineering at the University. He drops in every now and again.”

“Did any of the other customers look as if they were keeping an eye on Carson?”

“Muggers don't inhabit this pub,” he insisted. “I'd

spot them and have them out in no time at all."

"What sort of clientèle do you have here?" I enquired.

"One of the best in Edinburgh. We get a lot of the financial people coming in as well as business men and lawyers. People from the offices round about. And, of course, one or two students from the University. And, in the summer, we get a hell of a lot of tourists."

"So you have no idea who would have had a go at Carson?"

"None at all," he said. "My guess is that it was just a druggie looking for money for a score and who hit on the first guy to pass him."

I was inclined to agree with his analysis, so I headed for Fettes and let Sergeant Anderson have my report.

The next morning, I, as usual, reported to Chief Inspector Ian Forsyth on the results of the team's activities of the previous day, and finished by mentioning what I had had to deal with the previous evening. He was silent for a few minutes and then surprised me by saying that, if I had nothing better to do, I should join him for a drink and for something to eat at Casey's Bar that lunchtime.

"Do you know something about Casey's Bar or young Carson that I don't?" I asked.

"I know exactly what you do," he answered. "I believe that it might be interesting to pursue the mugging of Carson a little further."

I could see no reason why he should find a simple mugging so interesting. But I knew better than to query the maestro's judgement and agreed to pick him up at noon.

When we got to the pub not long after the start of the afternoon, we settled down at two stools at the bar counter and Forsyth ordered two Glenlivet malt whiskies for us. Murphy put the drinks in front of us and, having recognised me from the previous evening, asked if I had come to ask further questions related to the mugging of Carson. I introduced the Chief and indicated that he had other questions to ask. Murphy obviously had heard of Forsyth and looked at him with something approaching awe.

"How many people were still in the bar last night at the time that Carson decided to leave?" the Chief asked.

"I would reckon that there were about twenty-five

still here," Murphy replied.

"All of them known to you?"

"Most but not all."

"When Carson bought his last drink, did he pay with a note?"

Murphy screwed up his face in thought as he tried to recollect what had happened.

"Aye. I'm pretty sure that he paid with a twenty pound note."

"And you gave him a ten pound and a five pound note and some coins in change," Forsyth went on, "and it was these notes that were taken in the mugging?"

"That would be right."

There was a slight pause before Forsyth continued with his questioning.

"Have you any idea who it was who paid in these notes?"

"It could have been any one of them that were in the bar last night."

"Did anyone leave the bar in the ten minutes before Carson left or immediately after his departure?" the Chief enquired.

Again Murphy screwed up his face as he

thought.

"I'm pretty sure that no-one followed him out," he said. "There were four people who left shortly before Carson, Ewan Halliday, who is a banker, Bill Mercer, who is a businessman, Jim Calder, who works in one of the offices near here and a fellow I'd never seen before who had a couple of beers and then left."

"That one sounds like the man we want," I suggested.

Forsyth ignored my comment.

"Did Carson talk to anyone while he was here?" he asked.

"He probably exchanged a few words with people he knew, but he didn't spend time with anyone else."

"And did anyone seem to be paying particular attention to him while he was in here?"

"Not that I noticed."

Forsyth thanked him for his help and we ordered some food. While we were waiting for it, I asked the Chief whether the question and answer session had been productive.

"Who can tell at such an early stage?" he answered. "As you well know, only time can let you know whether the information you have collected will bear fruit or not “

We discussed other matters of interest for the rest of the time that we were there and returned to Fettes after we had eaten.

It was two days later that I was rung up by Sergeant Anderson from the front desk at Fettes.

“Alistair,” he said, “am I right in believing that you came across a man called Jim Calder while you were investigating that mugging a couple of days ago in Rose Street?”

Anderson reads assiduously all the reports that we make of incidents and has a very impressive memory.

“You are absolutely right,” I assured him. “What has Calder been involved in now?”

“He has gone and got himself murdered,” he told me. “I thought that you might wish to be the team that looks into the case.”

“Forsyth will certainly wish to. For some reason he saw a lot more in the mugging in Rose Street than I did.”

“That is why he is a Chief Inspector and you are only a lowly sergeant,” he pointed out somewhat offensively.

I sent the rest of the team on ahead to the crime scene and went to tell the Chief that, whatever it was that had aroused his interest in the mugging, it had been amply justified.

When I informed Forsyth that Calder had been murdered, he made no comment. We went down to the car and I paid little attention as he rolled himself into a ball and shot himself sideways into the car. But I put out a hand to keep him from squashing me against the driver's door and waited while he belted himself in before starting off. Once we were out into the traffic, I tried to find out whether he had anticipated something like this occurring.

"Did you foresee something further happening after the mugging?" I asked.

"I did not anticipate a murder," he admitted.

He was silent for a few moments and then decided to be frank.

"You may like to know that I have been active in the last couple of days. I managed to take photographs of all the people, apart from the one that Mr Murphy did not know, who left Casey's bar shortly before Carson departed."

I was a bit staggered that Forsyth had bothered to do a spell of hard graft out on the streets. He normally leaves all that to the rest of us. I had had no idea that he had not been in the Fettes building. The team had been involved in a case that had kept us menials all out and around in Edinburgh. But, since it was a case that had no intellectual content but involved only foot slogging and routine enquiries, Forsyth had not been involved. So I had had no clue that he had been doing some investigating on his own. And, in addition, I could see no reason why he would have bothered to do so.

"And what was the purpose of all this unusual activity?" I enquired.

"I wished to show these photographs to Mr Carson."

"For what purpose?"

"To see if he recognised one of them."

"And he might well have done so, since they had all been in the pub in Rose Street at the same time as he was there."

"I wished to see," he explained patiently, "if he recognised any of them as the man who had found him and called the ambulance."

"And did he?"

"The good Samaritan who tended him until the ambulance came was Jim Calder."

"Who has now been murdered."

"Precisely."

I thought about it.

"So you think that Calder knew more than we had guessed?" I suggested. "You think that he saw who it was who had done the mugging and that he has now been silenced to stop him revealing that information to us?"

"I do not think anything of the sort."

I was completely mystified.

"Then what do you think?"

"A minor league thief who would go to jail for a couple of months for a mugging," Forsyth pointed out. "is unlikely to risk going to jail for life for a murder done to conceal such a minor infringement."

"So what are you trying to tell me?"

"That it was Calder who actually did the mugging of Carter. But, since he wished his victim no real harm, he summoned the ambulance and waited with him to make sure he was all right until the medics arrived."

"But why on earth would Calder wish to rob a student like Carson?" I asked plaintively. "It doesn't make any sense."

"You are absolutely correct," he said. "It makes no sense that Calder, who had been in the bar and seen the clientèle, would mug a poor student when there were much better pickings to be had by mugging one of the more wealthy men, no doubt loaded with money and with expensive watches, very well worth stealing."

I was feeling even more lost.

"So why did he pick on Carson?"

"Because he clearly wanted to retrieve either the ten pound note or the five pound note that Carson had been given in his change when he purchased a drink in the bar."

"And why would he want to do that?" I asked, still plaintively. "What was so special about these notes?"

"That we do not yet know. But we can make a guess," he suggested. "One or other of them may have been stolen in a bank-raid or given in ransom in a kidnapping, in either case the numbers having been noted. Or it may have been counterfeit, but was not supposed to have been put out into the community and used to make a purchase until some date in the future."

Light was beginning to dawn.

"So you think," I said, "that Calder was a member of the gang involved. But that he helped himself to that note as a souvenir against the express instructions of the gang boss? And that he then inadvertently used that particular note to buy a drink in the bar. And, having realised what he had done, made sure he kept an eye on who got that note and made sure he got it back by clobbering Carson and retrieving it. And that the gang leader has now had him topped for disobeying instructions."

"But how do you suppose that the gang leader was able to become aware that Calder had helped himself to one of the notes and had then almost compromised them by using it for a purchase?" enquired Forsyth.

"How indeed?" I said thoughtfully. "Calder would certainly not say a word about the mess that he had almost made of things."

"So the gang must already have been a trifle suspicious of Calder and been keeping a watch on him," suggested the Chief.

He looked at me enquiringly.

"The fellow in the bar whom Murphy had never seen before," I said excitedly, "and who left about the same time as Calder, must have been the gang's spy. He saw everything that happened and reported back to his boss."

"So you had better detail one of the people from the lab to call on Murphy in the Rose Street bar and get him to make up a photofit picture of the person we now believe to have been the one who peached on Calder."

"I will certainly do that."

I spent the rest of the journey thinking about what Forsyth had just revealed to me. It certainly made the case a lot more interesting.

Calder had shared a flat in a tenement in Dalry with two other young men. The area around the tenement was occupied by a crowd of media representatives and sightseers, all kept in some sort of control by a couple of uniforms. These made a way through the throng for us and I parked the car near to the entrance to the tenement. The flat was on the second floor and we trudged our way up the stone steps to the landing from which the flat that Calder had occupied was reached. DC Andy Beaumont was waiting for us in the entrance.

Andy is a little on the short side for a policeman but he has two qualities that make him invaluable to the Force. The first is that he can pass for an average Joe anywhere. Once he's left you, you find it difficult to think of any characteristic with which to describe him. He can melt into a crowd and find out what's going on without anyone giving him a second glance. His build is average and he has an ordinary, unmemorable, innocent face, mousy brown hair and clothes indistinguishable from his neighbour's.

His second great virtue is that he could worm information from a tailor's dummy. When you talk to him, you get the impression that he's drinking in every word and that what you are saying is the most important thing in the world. He's the perfect listener and that, allied to his ready sympathy and ordinary appearance, means that neighbours, tradesmen and servants open their heart to him when any other copper would find them silent and resentful. As soon as we knew more about the dead man, Beaumont would be let loose to pick up all the gossip about him and about all possible suspects.

"Morning, sir," he greeted the Chief. "The dead man is Jim Calder who shared this flat with two others, who are in the living room waiting to be interviewed by you. They were out to a party last night that Calder didn't go to and, when they came home a wee bit the worse for wear, went straight to their beds. They only found out that Calder was dead this morning when they couldn't rouse him. But he had been dead since earlier in the evening. And there's no sign of a break-in anywhere. So he let in whoever it was who killed him."

We proceeded to Calder's bedroom where we found not only the dead body of Calder lying on the floor but Doc Hay, the police surgeon, kneeling beside it and Bill Cochrane from Forensics busy looking for clues around the room. Hay looked up as we entered, rose up from the body and moved across to greet us. At the same time he removed from his pocket a cigar case from which he extracted one of the cheroots to which he was addicted, lit it up, took in a satisfying lungful of the smoke and was prepared to talk to us.

Hay, at that time, was in his late forties, a rotund figure who peered benevolently at the world through thick pebble spectacles. He was wearing the usual shapeless clothes and had, on his head, the battered old soft hat without which he was never seen. Rumour has it that he sleeps in these garments as well. He was reputed to have no interest in life other than medicine and the only thing that was alleged to stir his heart was the thrill of expectation at the moment when he had a knife poised to slice into the latest victim on his mortuary table. But he was one of the best quacks in the business and you could rely one hundred percent on what he told you about a victim.

“Not much mystery about what happened here,” he said. “When the poor bastard turned his back, the killer hit him on the head and then strangled him with an old length of picture cord. All done without any mess.”

Bill Cochrane now came in. Bill was a mild-mannered chap, on the small side, with a round, cheerful face and a mop of close cropped, brown hair above it. He wore an old jacket and off-the-peg trousers and was reputed never to miss anything of significance at a crime scene.

"And before you ask me," he said, "he seems to have left no prints around. Probably wore gloves. And there is no chance of tracing where the cord was bought. That kind is sold in almost every DIY store and this lot is not new and may have been around for years."

I had a look around the room. It was quite large. Against one wall was a bed, at the side of which was a chest of drawers and at the foot of which was a wardrobe. The adjoining wall held a window that looked out onto a back green that was in great need of some careful, loving attention. Against the wall opposite the one that held the bed was a bookcase that contained mainly paperbacks, most of them of detective stories, and a desk in front of which was a comfortable-looking swivel chair. On the wall above the desk were hung two pictures, reproductions of famous paintings. The one on the left was a copy of *The Hay Wain*, the one on the right *Vase with Twelve Sunflowers*. The fourth wall, which contained the door by which we had entered the room, held a number of garish posters.

Forsyth had a quick tour of the room and I followed him round but neither of us found anything of interest.

“We had better have a word with the other two people who live here,” he said. “They may have some idea of the person with whom Calder has been frequenting.”

The flat contained, besides the three bedrooms and a bathroom, a large living room attached to which was a small kitchen. The other two occupants of the flat were sitting awkwardly in the living room under the watchful eye of a stolid uniform. We discovered that their names were Alan Benson and Colin Dawson. We sent Dawson off to his bedroom, along with the uniform, so that Forsyth and I could interview Benson alone.

“Have you any idea why someone would want to murder your friend?” I asked when the other two had left.

“Not really,” replied Benson. “Mind you, he was very keen to hit the big time and didn't mind what means he used to get there. So maybe he got mixed up in something too big for him.”

"Tell us the main people with whom he was involved in the course of his normal life," suggested Forsyth.

"He worked for a firm called Henderson and Foster, mainly for a man called Martin Heslop. He often met him outside working hours. Then all of us were members of a fitness club called Muscles Inc. He sometimes did the odd job for the man who ran the place, Billy Easton. He was also a member of a snooker club here in Dalry. I always thought that the man who owned it, with whom Calder was very friendly, a man called Robin Constable, was a bit of a rogue."

"And I gather that you and Dawson went to a party last night," I came in, "but that Calder didn't go with you."

"He said that he had some business to attend to, but that he would probably look in later."

"But he didn't join you at the party?"

"It looks as if he was dead long before he would have come to the party."

"And you didn't spot anything out of the ordinary when you got home from the party?"

"To be quite honest," Benson confessed, "we

were feeling pretty happy and a bit tired when we got back here and weren't noticing all that much. We just had this great desire to get to bed. Not that there was anything to see," he added. "We didn't spot anything amiss this morning until we went into his room to see why he hadn't surfaced."

We got nothing else of interest out of him and sent him to his bedroom while we interviewed Dawson. What we learned from him was a repeat of what we had already got from Benson. We had given up hope of getting anything fresh until we were on the point of taking our leave. It was at that stage that he added something new.

"Calder and I were at school together," he told us, "so I was closer to him than Benson was. That was probably why he gave me a message to pass on to you lot should anything ever happen to him. Mind you, I don't know whether he was being serious or not. He was well known as a bit of a joker. And the message doesn't make any sense."

Any message to us from a murder victim was well worth having.

"You had better tell us what the message was anyway," I suggested.

"He said to tell you P45."

"P45?" I said. "What the hell is that supposed to mean?"

"I have no idea. I told you that he was a bit of a joker. He was also into puzzles. He loved to have people racking their brains to work things out. I guess he meant for you lot to get your thinking caps on and deduce what it meant."

"Had Calder recently changed jobs?" I asked. "Maybe he was trying to indicate to us somebody from his previous employment who had a grudge against him."

"He has been in the same job ever since he left school. He has therefore never had to be given a P45."

When he had gone back to his bedroom, I looked across at Forsyth.

"The only P45 that I know about," I said, "is the government tax document, *Details of Employee Leaving Work*. In slang, it is also a phrase used to indicate 'termination of employment'. What on earth has any of that to do with the reason why someone has been murdered?"

"It is not immediately obvious what the

connection is," he admitted reluctantly.

DC Sid Fletcher now joined us. He had been going round the other flats in the tenement trying to find someone who had heard anything untoward during the previous evening or who perhaps had seen who had visited the murdered man's flat. Sid is a tall, lean, cadaverous individual, forty years old and with a gloomy expression and thinning, black hair. He's been the longest of all of us on Forsyth's team and will remain there till retirement. His many years in the force have convinced him that it will always be his fate to be the one left holding the short straw, and his wife leaving him, unable to stand the amount of time she was left on her own and the cold-shouldering by some of the neighbours, did nothing to lessen that view. But he carries on his work with fierce determination to show that he will not let the fates get him down. And he is fiercely loyal to Forsyth who is the one rock to which he can cling in the shifting sands of life. But he is also not the brightest of individuals.

"No-one in this block claims to have seen or heard anything last evening," he reported. "The whole lot of them might as well be deaf and blind. Of course, most of them probably have had run-ins with the police in the past and might well regard us as the enemy. In which case, they are not going to say a word to us even if they saw something."

"Some of the uniforms may have contacts with some of the locals," I suggested. "Get them to go round the area applying a bit of pressure. They may have more success than you, as an unwelcome stranger, might have."

I issued instructions to Andy and Sid as to what I wanted them to spend the rest of the day doing. Then I drove Forsyth back to Fettes, both of us immersed in thought during the journey. At Headquarters, I set up an incident room and wrote out a report of the morning's proceedings which I took up to Forsyth's office and handed over to him.

I found him immersed in thought, that giant brain trying to make sense of everything that we had heard and seen. He took the report and did no more than correct the grammar at one point and substitute at another a more felicitous phrase for one that I had used.

It was after I had left the Chief's office that I made my way into the centre of the city to do my part in the investigations that were needed if we were to get anywhere with the murder with which we had been landed.

CHAPTER 2

It was after five that evening before I got back to Fettes. I found Forsyth already gone for the day, so I wended my way to the pub where the team has a drink of an evening after a hard day's work. It lies halfway between Fettes and the Crematorium. I found Andy already there sitting at our usual table which is far enough from the bar counter and adjoining tables so that there is no risk that anything we say may find itself into flapping ears and appear in the next morning's *Scotsman* in garbled form.

Beaumont had a pint of heavy in front of him and I purchased the same at the bar and joined him at the table. We discussed a few matters of current interest until Fletcher arrived and joined us. It was only then that I turned the discussion to the current case. At that time Sandra Cockburn had just left us for higher things and we had not yet received an indication as to who was to replace her.

It may cause surprise that we were discussing the case in a pub and not in Headquarters with Forsyth in attendance, but it is common practice with us. Any team of Forsyth's that I run will always meet in the pub of an evening during the course of a major investigation in order to discuss the case. And there is a good reason why we do it in the friendly surroundings of a pub and not in the nick in the company of the great man.

Forsyth always plays his cards close to his chest. He suffered some little time ago an acrimonious divorce from his former wife, where lots of things that he had said came back in a form that told against him, and, probably because of that unedifying experience, he does not ever wish it to be known that he has said or done anything that might be considered to be wrong. And, having gone down that route, he has now got himself into a position where he wants to be regarded as infallible at all times. So he keeps his thoughts to himself until he is absolutely sure that he has got everything right and can prove it. In consequence, we mere mortals work for most of the time in the dark and follow normal procedure unless he condescends to come down from Mount Olympus and give us some instructions. These may, or may not, make sense, but we follow them to the letter. And later we discover why we were required to do these things and they all slot into place. But we never know what his thinking is until he has solved the case and is prepared to dazzle us all with the brilliance of his reasoning.

Most of those who work for Forsyth accept this philosophically, since his method of working has brought spectacular results. But, a few years previously, a rather bolshy Detective Constable on the team complained directly to him that he was unhappy at being treated like a cypher and kept totally in the dark. Forsyth's reply was simple. He pointed out that his method worked very successfully. So, only if one of his team arrived at the solution of a mystery before, or indeed even at the same time as, he did would he think of changing his *modus operandi.* He also added that, should such an unlikely event ever occur, he would proclaim the triumph of his minion from the rooftops and would also present the successful solver with a crate of the finest malt whisky.

Since that time, all teams have attempted to arrive at the solution of a major case before Forsyth is able to do so. This is not because we wish him to change his method of working which has been spectacularly successful, though a little more enlightenment during the course of an investigation would be very welcome. But we are intent on winning from him that crate of malt whisky in order to show him that, at least on one occasion, we can be every bit as brilliant as he is, and can beat him to the solution of a mystery. I have to confess humbly that so far we have not been able to achieve our strived-for ambition.

I began by letting the other two know everything that Forsyth and I had learned that morning. I always make sure that all members of any team I work with know everything that is being learned about a case. Some inspectors and sergeants keep the lower members of their squads completely in the dark, no doubt to reinforce their own positions. But the lowliest member of a team is as likely to come up with the brilliant idea that opens up and unwraps a case as is a grizzled veteran. But he cannot do that if the facts are withheld from him.

When I had finished, I went on to describe what I had learned that day. I had been trying to find out all that I could about the firm Henderson and Foster for whom Calder had worked.

"It is a firm," I told them, "that gives people advice on financial matters and helps them with tax problems. Since Calder was not particularly well qualified, he was a fairly lowly member of the organisation. But, since he was eager to get on, he was prepared to do whatever his superiors wanted, in and out of office hours. In particular, he did a lot of work on the side for one of his immediate bosses called Martin Heslop. Heslop is a *bon viveur* who drinks a lot and doesn't seem to take any exercise, so he has allowed himself to go to seed and is now so fat that he is quite gross. So he probably needs someone to do his leg work. Heslop has been involved in a number of dodgy financial deals in the past but has never fallen foul of the law. So it is not impossible that Heslop and Calder were involved in something not entirely kosher in the recent past that involved marked or counterfeit banknotes. But I could find no evidence that either had been linked with any past or ongoing crime."

I had a swallow of beer and asked Andy how he had got on. He put down his glass and started his account.

"I was finding out what I could about Muscles Inc," he explained. "It is quite a well regarded fitness club that seems to be doing well. It has quite an extended customer base. The chap who runs it, one

Billy (Slugger) Easton, used to be quite a well-known boxer, but he had a bad motor accident which finished his career and left him needing to use sticks. He is known to have contacts with people in the criminal world, and it is alleged that he has been into a few dicky ventures in his time. Since he is into a number of schemes outwith the fitness business, he has a number of people who do occasional jobs for him. One of these was Calder. It is not entirely clear what all these schemes entail, but you can bet your boots that some of them are a bit outside the law. But, as far as I could find out, he has never been done for illegal activities."

He picked up his glass and I signalled to Sid to carry on with the reports.

"I was looking into the Dalry Snooker Club," he told us. "It is run by a gentleman called Robin Constable, who has a bit of a temper which he finds it difficult to control. So he has crossed swords with a number of people and is by no means the most popular of gents. But it is rumoured that you can get a lot more at the club than a turn at the tables. Constable is alleged to be a fence who is prepared to acquire for any of his customers almost anything that they might desire. It's said that he will get involved in anything that will bring him in money. And Calder is one of the people who has done work for him in the past."

He stopped and drained his glass before setting off for the bar counter to set up another round. When he had returned, I sampled the new brew and then commented on what we had learned.

"So any of Heslop, Easton or Constable might well be into the crime that has caused Calder to be killed."

"In other words," said Fletcher, "today's work has not got us anywhere."

"It is early days yet," I pointed out. "I sent Bill Giles to the bar in Rose Street to produce a photofit picture of the unknown who was keeping an eye on Calder the time that Carson got mugged. I picked up three copies of the picture he has produced so as to be able to give each of us a copy tonight. Tomorrow we go back to where we each were today and flash the picture around. Let's see if anyone at one of these three places recognises him. That would give us a boost to trying to find which of the people we discussed tonight might have set him on to watching

Calder and, at a later stage, once the spy had reported, wanting him dead."

The other two had a look at the photofit pictures that I had passed over to them. Neither could remember seeing the fellow shown before. I bought another round and we spent a little time discussing other matters before we broke up.

I went off the next morning and showed the photofit picture to a number of people who worked for Henderson and Foster. After that I returned to Fettes and waited for Beaumont and Fletcher to turn up. When they did, and I had learned what they had found out, I went up to Forsyth's office, As always, he greeted me courteously and invited me to sit down.

"The three of us," I explained, "have been out this morning showing around the photofit of the fellow whom we believe was keeping an eye on Calder in the pub on the night when he did the mugging of Carson. We thought that, if he was known in one of the places that Calder frequented, that would give us a clue as to which of the establishments is involved in whatever got Calder killed."

"So what was the result of your enquiries?" he asked.

“The fellow's name is MacAllam. He appears to be a small time crook. Unfortunately, it turns out that he is well known in all three of the places. He had done work in the past for all of Heslop, Easton and Constable.”

“So you believe that we are no further forward,” he said.

“It looks that way.”

“Leave it with me,” he said. “I may be able to think of something.”

I suppose that I ought to finish the chapter by saying a bit more about the two major players in the drama, ie Forsyth and me. Forsyth is an imposing figure, an adjective that can also be applied to the way in which he deals with the hired help. He is 6’ 4” with a large-boned, quite athletic frame which he keeps in reasonable nick with exercise and golf. A shock of blonde hair stands up above the broad forehead that crowns his long, rather distinguished face and a luxuriant moustache adorns, to be kind about it, his upper lip.

Forsyth was born somewhere in the Highlands to a reasonably well-off family, and was educated at an exclusive public school in Edinburgh and then at the University there. He was married at quite an early age but the union didn't turn out too well and ended, as I have said, in an acrimonious divorce. This may explain his secretiveness and his unwillingness to leave himself open to criticism or to be shown to be in the wrong in any matter. He now lives alone, very well looked after by a housekeeper who is not only competent but an excellent cook. He enjoys a social life that includes golf at one of the more exclusive courses, bridge at one of the local clubs in Edinburgh, concerts and the theatre and allows him to mix with the great and the good in the higher echelons of Edinburgh society. We don't see all that much of him outside working hours though we are invited round to his house in a fairly exclusive area of Edinburgh for dinner from time to time and are always well looked after, superbly fed and supplied with a sufficiency of excellent wine and spirits.

It is not clear why Forsyth chose the police force as a career. He would have succeeded at almost any job he had decided to pursue. It is also difficult to imagine how he endured the years as a humble footslogger without resigning in frustration or being thrown out on his ear by outraged superiors, or how he ever achieved promotion to his present elevated rank. It is probable that in these days he had not yet acquired his later arrogance and was more prepared to conform and to turn that massive intellect to trivial and uninspiring tasks. Legend has it that one of his more perceptive superiors recognised his qualities and took the trouble to steer him gently through the troubled waters to his present safe and well-fitting niche.

It says much for the Lothian and Borders Police that they are prepared to put up with a Chief Inspector who is bored by ninety percent of his job and, in consequence, is worse than useless at it, in order to have him available when the other ten percent appears on the scene. I suppose that it also says much for the squads whom he has commanded that they are also prepared to put up with him. Not that those at the bottom of the pile in any police force have much say in their fate. Though those of us who work under him often resent being landed with jobs he should be doing, as well as our own, and spend a good deal of our time taking the mickey when he's at his most infuriating or arrogant, we would defend him to the death against any outsider. He has pulled too many chestnuts out of the fire for us in the past and, despite the appalling conceit of the man in assuming that we will be delighted to do, without a murmur of dissent, all the hard graft he should be tackling himself, we know that he has fought for us when we have got into trouble and always makes sure that we share in the credit when he has cracked one of the big ones. We have a real love-hate relationship with him but no-one has ever asked to be shifted from his squad to another.

As to me, I was born in Edinburgh and spent my early years in a tenement flat off Dundee Street. My father worked in a nearby brewery, of which Edinburgh at that time had more than its fair share, but he was killed in an accident at work when I was just eight years old. The firm did well by us according to their lights and the mores of the times. They gave the family a tiny pension and my mother a job serving food to the bosses in their canteen. As a result, we managed to live reasonably comfortable lives in comparison with many others in the area though money was always a bit on the tight side. And, since I was now the orphaned son of an Edinburgh burgess, I was eligible to became a Foundationer at George

Heriot's School.

George Heriot, Jinglin' Geordie as Sir Walter Scott called him in his novel, was a goldsmith in the reign of James VI of Scotland. He made a pretty good living at his craft, but an even better one from lending money to the King and the courtiers who were always in need of a ready source of cash. When the sovereign became James 1 of the newly-formed Great Britain and moved to London, Heriot went with him. Since the need for ready money was even greater there for a king and nobles living well beyond their means, Geordie found himself coining in the readies hand over fist. Since he had no heirs when he died, he left his money to found a school for the orphans of the Edinburgh citizenry.

The trustees were shrewd Scots businessmen who invested the money wisely. The Trust grew and prospered. More than a century ago the school expanded and opened its doors to all the sons of Edinburgh who could afford the fees, the Foundationers no longer boarding in the school building but receiving an allowance to stay elsewhere and attend the school, like the rest, as day pupils. I was one of these, staying at home with my mother during the night but mixing with the sons of the well-to-do middle classes on an equal footing during the day. I acquired not only a sound education but an insight into a life far removed from that enjoyed by my mother.

While I did well enough in exams, I was never one of the high flyers. Although I was urged by some of the teachers at the school to go on to university and take a degree, I knew that wasn't for me. Book learning I had had enough of. I wanted some hands-on experience. I was keen to go on learning, but in a job.

What led me to a career in the police I'm not sure. Perhaps it was the great respect for the law that my mother dinned into me. Or perhaps it was the lawlessness that I saw, and hated, in the jungle of tenements around where I lived. Since my mother refused point blank to leave the flat in which she had spent so much of her life and near which all her friends resided, and I didn't feel that I could desert her, my early years as a copper were not pleasant. My neighbours regarded me as a traitor to my roots and it was always uncomfortable when I was involved in any operation that impinged on the criminal occupations of the area. So, when my mother died, I moved as far away from the area as possible and bought a bungalow in Liberton on the southern outskirts of the city. I still had the odd friend in the district where I'd grown up, but we tended to meet in town on the increasingly fewer occasions on which we got together. When you're in the police and have come from a poor background, you have to make new friends to survive.

I got a transfer to the CID in due course and never looked back. Detective work proved to be my métier. I had a certain native intelligence and worked hard. I passed the sergeants' exams and got promoted. I hadn't been long a sergeant when I was informed that I was to be installed in Forsyth's squad, his previous sergeant having at last made it to the rank of Inspector, leaving behind a vacancy that had to be filled. I was initially flattered to be assigned to the team of a man with the kind of reputation that Forsyth had, since he was even then a bit of a legend, although I had heard that he could be a difficult man to work for. I soon found out that working for him was not likely to be a bed of roses and I was already somewhat disillusioned when the first murder case in which we were involved together came along. It was a pretty traumatic experience where the way in which Forsyth conducted the investigation almost gave me heart failure and where I feared at one time that my career in the police force was about to come to an ignominious end. I have chronicled these never to be forgotten events in a story entitled *The Crime Committee.* Fortunately, it turned out all right in the end and we became an established team.

These traumatic events that formed the beginning of our work as a team explain the odd relationship that I have with Forsyth. When you have seen Forsyth at his best and also at his worst, totally ignoring the rules of how a crime should be investigated, you find yourself a little short in the tugging of the forelock mentality. And, to give Forsyth his due, he is not much into believing that Inspectors are a different species from the lower ranks.

CHAPTER 3

It was three days later that I was called up at home in the evening by Sergeant Anderson who informed me that a young man called MacAllam had been found murdered. Since Anderson assiduously reads all the reports that the detective teams produce, he was aware that the Forsyth team had had dealings with the man in the past. He suggested to me that we should take on board the latest incident in the ongoing saga. I told him to get Beaumont and Fletcher to the scene and went out to get the car and pick up Forsyth.

MacAllam had lived in a flat in a multi-storey block of flats situated on the fringes of Sighthill. As we were driving there after I had picked him up, Forsyth, who had been looking a trifle shifty, finally broke the silence.

"I am afraid that I might be the person responsible for the death of this young man," he confessed.

"How could you have caused such a thing to happen?" I asked.

"I sought out MacAllam and had a session with him. The enquiries that you three made about him must have drawn him to the attention of the person who is running the crime into which we are looking. As a consequence, I imagine that he has had someone keeping an eye on MacAllam. When he was informed that I had had an interview with him, I assume that he also had a session with MacAllam, found out what had passed between the two of us and decided that MacAllam was too much of a threat to his future to be allowed to continue living."

"But how could anything that he said to you be a threat to his boss's existence?" I asked. "Did you manage to bribe him to reveal all?"

"It was not necessary for me to bribe him. When I told him who his boss was and that I knew that it was that person who had ordered the killing of Calder, he felt it prudent to tell me all he knew in the hope that he would not be charged as an accessory after the fact."

I was staggering under the impact of the news that Forsyth was telling me.

"But how could you tell him who his boss was?" I enquired.

"Because I had managed to deduce what the cryptic message about P45 meant," he said.

"So what does it mean?" I asked.

I should have known that he was not going to reveal at that moment anything that would detract from the impact that his eventual revelation would be intended to produce.

"My interpretation of the cryptic message may be wrong," he suggested. "I would not wish to set your thinking in the totally wrong direction."

"But how can your thinking be wrong if MacAllam was scared enough by your revelations to reveal various matters to you?"

"If I had got it wrong, MacAllam may have thought it prudent to go along with my misconception and tell me a lot of made-up lies."

I sighed and accepted the fact that I was not going to prise any of his secrets from him.

"So did MacAllam reveal sufficient things to you that would allow you to put a case to the Procurator Fiscal?" I asked.

"Unfortunately not," he admitted. "He was not high enough up in the hierarchy to have evidence that would stand up in court. And the suppositions of a dead man are not something to which a jury would pay much attention."

We were silent for the rest of the journey, each immersed on his own thoughts. When we got to our destination in Sighthill, we found a large crowd around the multi, made up mostly of locals but with a few members of the press and television mixed in. The uniforms who were keeping an eye on the mob cleared a path for us and I parked the car close to the entrance to the block. The lift, needless to say, was out of order and we had to trudge our way up two flights of stairs, that smelled strongly of urine and were embellished with some not very artistic graffiti, before we got to the flat that MacAllam had inhabited. Andy was awaiting our arrival in the entrance lobby as usual.

"Evening, sir," he greeted the Chief. "The dead man is the same MacAllam who was the subject of the photofit picture that we recently made some enquiries about. It looks as if he let his killer in, but was suspicious enough as to what was about to happen to have been able to put up a bit of a struggle. Not that it did him any good in the end."

"Who found the body?" I enquired.

"Apparently someone made an anonymous 999 call to report a disturbance in this flat. The uniforms who came to investigate broke in when they could get no response to their knocking and found the dead man. You will find that the doc and Bill Cochrane are in the sitting room with the body."

There was a tiny linoleum covered hall from which led off a sitting room, a bedroom, a bathroom and a kitchen. The sitting room was not large and had a floor that was covered with cheap carpeting. The room contained a sofa, and an armchair that had been knocked over, facing a television set mounted on a stand. A further small table, that had held a lamp, a Scrabble board and tiles, had been been knocked over and the tiles were scattered widespread around the room. There was also a drinks cabinet against one wall which, when we examined it, displayed an interesting collection of cans and bottles of booze. There were signs, by the marks showing on the carpet, that a scuffle had taken place. The body of MacAllam lay near the corner of the room. He appeared to have dragged himself there in order to set up some of the scrabble tiles. What he had produced read 'boss'.

Dr Hay was kneeling beside the body and Bill Cochrane was examining a couple of glasses that stood on a small table near the sofa. Hay saw us enter the room and rose from his position beside the body, uttering a few groans as he did so and remarking that it was hell to be growing old. He came to meet us, removing from his pocket as he did so his cigar case, from which he removed one of the cheroots that it contained. Once he had lit this and had had a satisfying lungful of the smoke produced, he greeted us affably.

“This one,” he then said, “seems to have been a bit suspicious of the fellow he had let in. So he put up a bit of a resistance when his visitor turned nasty. As you can see, a few things got knocked over in the struggle. But, in the end, he got hit over the head and then strangled while he was out cold. But the killer didn't do a particularly good job and the victim was still not quite dead. So he was able, after the killer had left, to crawl painfully over to the spilled tiles and leave you a message.”

“Didn't the noise they made as they struggled bring any of the neighbours to see what was happening?” I enquired.

“In this place, you don't poke your nose into other people's business,” Hay pointed out, “or you might get it put out of joint. If someone is having a set-to with a partner or someone collecting a debt, you don't get involved or you get your head kicked in as well."

"Charming people," I observed.

I turned to Cochrane.

"If they were having a drink together before the violence erupted," I said, "are there any prints that would be useful to us on the glasses?"

"I'm afraid not," he said. "Both glasses have been wiped clean."

I looked back at the message that MacAllam had left and turned to Forsyth.

"It doesn't really help us," I pointed out, "to be told that MacAllam was killed by his boss. Which one of the three is he referring to? Why didn't he give us the killer's name?"

"He was on the edge of death," said the Chief gently. "It must have required quite an effort to drag himself over to the tiles. And, when he got there, he would have to do what he could with the tiles that were at hand. At least his effort lets us know that it was the boss who killed him. He had not delegated the task to one of his henchmen."

I realised that I had been churlish in denegrating MacAllam's efforts to leave us a clue

"I guess we should be grateful that he made the effort to tell us what he could," I said.

We found nothing else of interest in the sitting room. When we went into the bathroom, we found that the medicine cabinet was open and, beneath it, lay a tin that had contained Bandaids with what had been its contents scattered around it on the floor. Nearby lay a couple of the transparent pieces that had at one time covered the sticky portions on one of the Bandaids.

"So our killer got damaged by MacAllam in the fight," I said, "and had to use a Bandaid to prevent traces of his blood being left at the scene. I will make sure that Cochrane looks for any trace of blood that's not MacAllam's, though I'm sure the killer will have cleaned up any trace that there might have been. And we will certainly be examining all our suspects to see if any of them has recently suffered from a cut or any wound that would have bled."

We went into the bedroom. It was a warm night and the window was open at the bottom. The room contained a bed, a chest of drawers, a bedside table and little else. There were racks on the wall where MacAllam had hung his clothes. The bed, an old one which had wheels on the end of its legs so that it could be moved easily, stood in the middle of the wall opposite the window. I looked at the marks on the carpeting at the side of the bed and then examined the floor more closely.

"The bed has been moved recently," I pointed out.

Forsyth came across and joined me in looking at the area around the bed. I went down on my knees and examined the area more completely. I even lifted up the carpeting, which came up quite easily. There was nothing hidden underneath it. When I got up again, I was puzzled.

"I thought that MacAllam might have hidden something, such as an illicit banknote, in a hiding place in the wall or the skirting board or under the carpeting," I suggested, "and that the killer might have moved the bed to get at it. But there is no evidence of any hiding place down there, though I suppose that the killer might have removed something that had been hidden by MacAllam under the carpet."

"Have you noticed an even more curious item?"

asked Forsyth. “The two legs at the head of the bed have been tied to the wall radiator by a couple of leather belts.”

I looked and what he had said was correct. Belts connected the bed legs to the radiator.

“Why on earth would anyone want to do that?” I asked.

Forsyth made no comment. I examined the area more closely and realised that there had obviously been subsidence in the block of flats and that the bedroom floor sloped slightly down from the opposite wall to where the bed had originally stood. I tucked that fact away in my mind.

The Chief had prowled around the room and stopped to have a look at the window. I joined him. It was a dark night, but one could just about see that the window looked out on to a small grassed area behind the flats that separated the building from the trees that marked the edge of the area of council housing. I noted that the dirt on the sill outside the window had been disturbed as if something had been dragged across it.

We had a look into the kitchen but found nothing there of interest. As we were about to leave, I asked

Forsyth if anything that we had seen suggested matters of interest to him. He thought carefully before answering.

“I believe that MacAllam's message,” he said at length, “allied to the spilled Bandaids and the altered position of the bed may allow us to bring the case to a successful conclusion.”

“So you have solved the case by using logical deduction,” I suggested. “But do you also have the necessary concrete evidence that will convince the Procurator Fiscal that you have a case that he can take to court?”

“I believe that I should be able to obtain such evidence during the course of tomorrow.”

As we walked into the hallway, we found that Fletcher had arrived. He reported that no-one in the block claimed to have heard a peep out of MacAllam's flat during the evening.

“Some, if not all, of them are lying of course,” he pointed out. “There must have been quite a din in here as they struggled. But, in a place like this, you don't poke your nose into the affairs of others. And you don't give the police, who are the enemy, any help at all.”

I let Forsyth go ahead out to the car. I told the other two that I wanted each of us to interview the boss that he had looked into some days ago. Each of them would, no doubt, have an alibi for this evening, but we should insist on seeing whether any of them had a Bandaid covering a cut somewhere on his body, getting them to strip down to their boxers, if necessary. Thereafter, I suggested that we all met at my house in Liberton.

It was much later that I drove into the street where I live in Liberton. I could see that the cars of the other two were parked a little way from my house under a street lamp. By the time that I had put my car into its garage, the pair had emerged from Sid's car and were waiting by the front door for my arrival. I ushered them into the sitting room, sat them down, opened three cans of McEwans, added to these three whisky chasers and we all had a drink of both brews before I started the proceedings.

I told them everything that Forsyth and I had come across that evening, and informed them that Forsyth had solved the crime and hoped to have the concrete evidence that would have the Procurator Fiscal jumping for joy later in the day that was shortly about to dawn.

"So you are saying," said Beaumont, "that, unless we can come up with a solution here and now, that case of malt whisky will once again have eluded us."

"That is the situation," I agreed. "Now it seems that what led Forsyth to the solution was his ability to deduce what the P45 reference meant. Have any of you had any thoughts about what Calder was trying to tell us?"

Both shook their heads glumly and I felt that I could safely put forward the idea that had come to me on the subject.

"When does somebody get given a P45?" I asked.

"When he's left work," said Fletcher.

"Precisely!" I said. "When he's left work. Hes, I for left, op for work leads us to Heslop."

There was a startled silence which was broken by Beaumont.

"That's brilliant," he said. "And it's just the sort of thing that a puzzle freak like Calder would come up with."

"And you might like to know that Heslop, when I

interviewed him a short while ago was sporting a Bandaid on his cheek. He claimed that he had cut himself shaving that morning, but he would say that, wouldn't he, if he had been cut by MacAllam in the fight in the flat."

"And I didn't find a cut anywhere on Easton," said Beaumont.

"Nor did I find one on Mr Constable," added Fletcher.

"What about all the things that Forsyth drew attention to after the events of last evening?" asked Beaumont. "Does your theory answer all the Chief's worries?"

"Heslop is one of the bosses we were looking into," I pointed out, "so MacAllam was naming him with the message with the tiles. The only one sporting a Bandaid is Heslop. As to the movement of the bed, I imagine that, after MacAllam had his session with Forsyth and found out that the net was closing in on Heslop and whatever the operation was that he was in process of running, he decided to take out insurance against the day when everything crashed down about his ears."

"And what insurance would that be?" enquired

Fletcher.

"He decided to get a hold of one of the notes that caused all the trouble to start when Carson lost his."

"And you think that he moved the bed and tied it in its new position," Beaumont came in, "so that he could get at the note, which he had hidden under the carpet in his room, in case Heslop got wind of the situation and he had to get out, with his insurance policy, fast?"

"Just so." I agreed. "And, since his bedroom floor sloped badly, he had tied the bed to the radiator to make sure that it didn't roll back to its previous position."

They sat and thought about it. It was Beaumont who spoke first.

"I like it," he said. "It all fits together and makes sense."

"So I present it to Forsyth tomorrow before he announces that the case is closed?"

When they agreed, I fetched three more cans of McEwans and refilled all the whisky glasses. It was a cheerful gathering that broke up a short while thereafter.

I was in early the next morning despite getting to bed so late, but Forsyth did not show. It was not until almost lunchtime that he put in an appearance. I allowed him time to get to his office and have a look at his mail before I bearded him in his lair.

He greeted me courteously as ever and, when I enquired as to whether he had got the necessary evidence to present his case to the Procurator Fiscal, replied in the affirmative.

"In that case," I said, "would you have the time to listen to a solution to the case that was arrived at by the team in the early hours of this morning?"

"I will always make time to hear one of your solutions," he replied. "It is always entertaining to see how your mind works."

He settled back comfortably in his chair, put the tips of his fingers together, closed his eyes and prepared to concentrate on my presentation. He sat unmoving during my discourse and remained that way for a few seconds after I had finished before he opened his eyes and smiled across at me. At that moment I knew that the solution that I had just expounded did not agree with the one at which he had arrived.

"Your solution," he said, "is most ingenious, as always."

"But it does not agree with the one that you have deduced?"

"I am afraid not. And I have to inform you that I have the evidence to prove to you, or indeed to anyone else, that my solution is the correct one to our mystery."

"So where did we go wrong?"

He thought for a few moments.

"Your explanation of the P45 clue, while ingenious, is a little too convoluted to be the sort of thing that a person worried about his future health was likely to leave for what he might well have regarded as the boneheaded police. However addicted to puzzles he might have been, he was likely to have left something more easily interpreted."

"Was that the only thing that we got wrong?" I asked.

"Far from it," he said gently. "Your interpretation of almost all the other clues that we found was well wide of the mark."

I felt thoroughly deflated.

"You will have to excuse me," he went on. "I

have a number of matters to attend to and then I will have to inform our superiors that the case is solved. Thereafter I will have to explain in detail my reasoning to the Chief Constable and to the Chief Super, which may take a little time since neither has a mind attuned to the niceties of logical reasoning. But I shall be buying drinks for the team at 5.30 this evening in the usual hostelry. And I can then explain to you more fully, should you wish, where it was that you went wrong in your reasoning."

And, with that, he was gone, leaving me, as was usual on these occasions, in a state of mixed emotions. It was excellent that another case had been brought to a successful conclusion. We would share in the glory that this would bring. But it was disheartening that, once again, we had failed to beat him to the punch. And it was infuriating that he had given me no clue as to the correct solution so that I could try to work it out for myself. But nothing should be done that would detract from the impact on us mere mortals that his revelation of the truth was supposed to produce.

And, as usual, I found the 'should you wish' amusing. The whole purpose of the meeting in the bar was to impress us with the brilliance of his reasoning. If we were to say, during the drinks session, that we did not wish to hear his exposition of the solution, I am sure that he would have tied us to our chairs so that we would have had to listen.

I sighed and went off to let the others know that we would be getting free drinks, and a lesson in logical reasoning, that evening.

All the facts necessary to deduce who killed Calder and MacAllam have now been given. If you decide to try to arrive at a solution before Forsyth reveals all, good luck to you.

Alistair MacRae

CHAPTER 4

Five-thirty found the three of us sitting at our usual table in the pub with pints of heavy on the table in front of us. In front of the place soon to be occupied by Forsyth stood a glass of his favourite malt whisky, Glenlivet. He will, in due course, buy drinks for us, more than one round if we are lucky and the proceedings are prolonged, but he expects a glass of Glenlivet to be awaiting his arrival.

He appeared in the doorway, stopped there and looked around. Since he knows perfectly well at which table we always sit, the pause is intended to allow the other denizens of the bar to see which celebrity it is who has decided to grace the place with his presence. Since he had not appeared on television for some time and drinkers tend to have short memories, his arrival caused no interest whatsoever. Undeterred, he moved over to our table, greeted us cheerfully, sat down, sampled the Genlivet and was now ready to start the proceedings that would make us be astonished by his brilliance.

"The Chief Constable is," he said, "as always, impressed with our ability to solve such a complex case so speedily and has asked that his heartiest congratulations should be passed on to you all."

"We didn't do all that much," I pointed out.

"You did your usual invaluable job of providing the necessary information without which the case could not have been solved."

He had another swallow of whisky before continuing.

"You came up with your usual attempt at a solution, which, unfortunately, was not the correct one. And one of the main reasons for this was that you did not correctly interpret the clues that were available at the scene of the final murder."

"I don't see how you could interpret the tile clue as anything but that one of the three bosses had done the murder,"said Beaumont belligerently.

"I agree," sad Forsyth. "But everything else you got wrong."

He had another swallow of whisky before resuming.

"You apparently did not find it strange," he resumed, "that the killer, having spilled the Bandaids out of the tin on to the floor of the bathroom, did not carefully return them to the tin when he had used one of them and then return the tin to the bathroom cabinet. Had he done so, we would have had no idea that the killer needed to cover up a cut. Surely even the most amateurish of criminals would have known enough not to leave such a clue for us and would have cleaned up accordingly."

"So you are saying that the killer planted the clue to mislead us?" suggested Fletcher.

"I am and you can see how well it worked. I imagine that the killer had run across Heslop that day and noted that he had a Bandaid on his face. That gave him the idea for the false clue."

Forsyth finished off the whisky in his glass and noted that all our glasses were empty. He asked Fletcher if he would be good enough to go to the bar counter and purchase large Glenlivets all round, something that Sid was only too happy to do. Forsyth handed him some notes for the purchase. When Fletcher had returned with the fresh drinks, the Chief resumed his discourse.

"Your explanation of the movement of the bed was also wide of the mark. Why would MacAllam not have left the bed in its normal position even if he had stashed something under the carpet beneath it?

Leaving the bed in its new position would have alerted anyone looking for a hiding place as to where he should explore. And, had MacAllam needed to get at the hiding place in a hurry, it would have taken only a moment to move the bed and access the carpet. And why would he have needed to tie the bed to the radiator?"

"The floor in the bedroom sloped," I said without much conviction.

"Not to the extent that the bed was likely to roll back to its original position."

"So why had the bed been moved?" asked Fletcher.

Forsyth ignored the question as he took a swallow from his glass.

"The killer would have waited," he said when he was able to talk again, "until he could slip up to MacAllam's apartment unseen by any of the occupants of the other flats. But if, as happened, MacAllam put up resistance, the commotion would have alerted the other dwellers there that something was amiss."

"But, as we saw," Beaumont pointed out, "no-one was likely to poke his nose in and see what was happening."

"I agree," sad Forsyth, "that no neighbour was likely to interfere. But some of them might well have kept an eye open to see who emerged from MacAllam's flat after the commotion had died down. Such knowledge might have been a source of money in the future."

"I guess you're right."

I am sure that Forsyth had to make an effort to restrain himself from pointing out that he was always right.

"Our killer is a careful man who plans ahead for such emergencies," he continued. "He had made preparations should the killing be noisy enough to attract the attention of others in the flats and had brought with him, no doubt wrapped around his body, a length of rope."

"The window being open and the sill showing signs of something having been dragged across it should have alerted us to that possibility," I said ruefully.

"And, if you are going to shin out of the window on a rope to the deserted area behind the flats," Forsyth pointed out, "you need to tie the rope to something."

"The bed being the obvious choice."

"And you have to make sure that the bed will not move by fastening it to the radiator."

"And once outside safely," I hazarded, "you release the slip knot that ties the rope to the bed, pull the rope down and carry it with you to your waiting car."

"And, since this had been the method of leaving the murder scene," the Chief pointed out, "it seemed to indicate who the killer had been. It seemed to me highly unlikely, if not impossible, that Heslop or Easton would have contemplated such a manoeuvre. One is far too fat, the other too lame, to be able to carry out such a manoeuvre successfully."

"But you already knew that the killer was Constable," I said, "You had cracked the meaning of P45."

"I had," he admitted, trying to look modest. "As you yourself pointed out P45 meant 'left work'. In Calder's bedroom, above the desk, were reproductions of two works of art. The left work was *The Hay Wain,* which was painted by John Constable. And one of the people for whom Calder did odd jobs was also called Constable."

It all made a satisfying whole and I was convinced that it was the truth but I had to make the point that it was all theorising.

"The Procurator Fiscal," I pointed out, "will need more concrete evidence before he will take the case to court."

"And, of course, I have such evidence to give him. On the strength of my deductions, I was able to persuade a magistrate, who understands and appreciates logic, to grant me a warrant and, armed with that, I and some uniformed policemen made a thorough search of the Snooker Club premises. In the basement, we found the necessary equipment to produce counterfeit ten pound notes and a large stack of such notes that had already been printed, ready for circulation into the marketplace. It would be very difficult for Constable and his cronies to wriggle out from under that."

"So another triumph has been added to the many already marked against your name," I said with genuine feeling.

He attempted to look modest with his usual lack of success.

“I am, unfortunately, scheduled,” he said, “to give an interview on the television shortly, so I shall be forced to leave you and make my way to the studio. But that should not prevent you from continuing to celebrate the team's latest success.”

He handed me another couple of notes, finished his Glenlivet, thanked us for joining him and made his way from the bar.

I went over to the counter and acquired another round of three large Glenlivets. There was still enough change left after the purchase to allow me to obtain three packets of crisps. I took everything back to the table. We opened the crisp packets, ate some and then sampled the new drinks. Each of us gave a satisfied sigh.

“There are a lot of worse things in this life,” I observed, “than being one of the members of Forsyth's team.”

“He can be a bit of bastard at times,” said Beaumont, “but he makes up for that at times like these.”

“I still think that he's the best boss that anyone could have,” said Fletcher defiantly.

And, with Glenlivet warming the cockles of our

hearts, none of us was going to disagree.

THE ISLAND OF DEATH

CHAPTER 1

The good looking young man drove his Jaguar over the rather rickety bridge that connected Mary's Island to the mainland in a remote part of south-east Scotland. It was the first time that he had been there and he was not impressed. The island was roughly circular with a diameter of just under half a mile and was devoid of trees. It had steep cliffs as its boundary for most of its circumference, the only exception being a small cove on the northern side where boats could land with some difficulty at a small jetty. The only building that the island held was a large stone-built house which stood roughly in its centre.

A tarmacked road ran from the bridge to the house, but it had not been resurfaced for some time and held a number of potholes which the driver had to be on the alert to avoid. He brought the car to a halt beside two others outside the front of the house and clambered from the driver's seat. There was a bitter wind blowing and the sky held the portents of the impending storm. He shivered. He was glad that he had got to his destination before the predicted storm broke.

The house had been built something like a century before and had no pretensions to being other than a straightforward dwelling house. It was square, without embellishment, was three storeys high and constructed from local stone.

As he made for the entrance, a man dressed in a dark suit emerged from the house and approached him.

"I assume that you would be Mr Stirling," he said.

"Well spotted," replied the new arrival.

"I am Watters. I am the butler here. Since all the other guests have already arrived, it was not difficult to tell whom you would be. I will show you to your room and, if you will be good enough to open your boot, I will bring your suitcase up with me."

Stirling pushed open the boot and Watters, with difficulty, removed the two large suitcases that the boot contained and carried them into the house with Stirling following behind.

The entrance hall was imposing. It was covered in wood panelling. There was in one wall a magnificent marble fireplace which contained a roaring fire, although the house was centrally heated. Above the fireplace was a stag's head with panels on either side carrying some kind of armorial bearing.

Pictures of hirsute worthies, no doubt ancestors of the present owner, adorned the walls, as well as landscapes of mountainous Scottish scenery. Two suits of armour stood guard near the foot of an ornate wooden staircase that led to the upper floors.

Watters mounted the staircase with Stirling close behind and the procession finished in a room halfway along the corridor on the first floor. The room was large with a high ceiling and the window gave a view of the bridge that Stirling had so lately crossed and the inhospitable land beyond on the mainland. The furniture in the room was old fashioned but comfortable. Watters deposited the suitcases beside the bed and informed Stirling that drinks would be served in the drawing room on the ground floor in around forty minutes, from six-thirty, prior to dinner being served at seven o'clock.

When the butler had departed, Stirling carefully hung up his jackets and trousers in the wardrobe and deposited his shirts, socks and underwear in the chest of drawers. The gun he concealed under the mattress. He then had a shower in the en suite bathroom that was attached to his bedroom, dressed in fresh clothes and made his way down to the drawing room. He was interested to notice as he descended the stairs that the storm had started and that there already appeared to be several inches of snow lying on the ground outside the house.

He was clearly the last of the guests to come down. There were already five people in the room. One of these, a middle-aged man of upright carriage, impeccably dressed and with well-groomed, silvery hair approached him.

"I am your host, Michael Conway," he said. "Let me welcome you to my humble home. What can I get you to drink? We have almost everything that you might desire."

"A malt whisky with a little spring water would be most acceptable," Stirling informed him.

They moved over to a table in the corner that held a wide variety of hard and soft drinks. Conway poured the drink for Stirling, handed it to him and then laid a hand on his arm.

"Let me introduce you to the others," he said.

The rather good looking woman, though with a certain hardness in her features, who appeared to be in her mid-twenties, turned out to be Cynthia Howard. She eyed Stirling with interest when he was introduced to her. She had been talking to a well-dressed man of about the same age, with an intellectual look, who was introduced as Allan Preston.

The other two guests standing together were a little older and were Alice Jardine and William MacIntyre. She had the look of an intellectual spinster and he struck Stirling as a bit of a con man. The five chatted with each other and with their host about various inconsequential matters, none of the guests being prepared to broach the subject of why they had been invited there.

The dinner, served by Watters and a young woman referred to as Mary, was excellent and was accompanied by some first class wines. It was only when they had returned to the drawing room, where they were served with coffee and further drinks that Conway decided to let them know why they had been invited to the island.

"You were all friends of my son, Martin," he announced. "You may, or may not, know that he committed suicide a few months ago. I felt that I wanted to meet his friends and I thought that it might be a suitable tribute to him that we should spend this extended weekend reminding ourselves of what a wonderful person he was and paying a tribute to his short but useful life."

There was a short, embarrassed silence while each of the guests made his or her assessment as to whether this was how he would wish to spend the next few days. But all of of them appeared to accept that, if the payment for a pleasant several days spent in comfortable surroundings and accompanied by good food and a sufficiency of alcohol, was to indulge an old man, then they were prepared to accept the conditions.

There was a short period spent cataloguing the merits of the younger Conway before the discussions moved to more general topics. A large amount of alcohol had been consumed by each of them before the group broke up and people starting making their ways upstairs to bed. Stirling noted, as he mounted the stairs, that the snow was no longer falling but that there were several inches of the white stuff covering the area around the house. He locked his door, cleaned his teeth, undressed and slipped into his bed. He slept a dreamless sleep.

He had not set his alarm and it was almost nine o'clock before he arose from his bed. He shaved, showered and dressed and was about to leave his room when there was an enormous explosion from somewhere outside the house. He rushed to the window where he saw that smoke was still arising from the bridge that led to the mainland. The central span of the bridge was missing, meaning that it would no longer be possible to get to the mainland by using that route.

After one horrified look at the scene, he rushed from the room and raced downstairs.

All the other guests, as well as Conway and Watters were standing dumbstruck outside the front door, staring at what was left of the bridge, trying to understand what had happened.

“What could have caused such an accident to the bridge?” asked Alice Jardine.

“There was nothing on the bridge that could have caused such an accident,” Stirling pointed out. “That section of the bridge was deliberately blown up.”

“But why would anyone want to destroy the bridge?”

“Why indeed. It does mean that we are trapped here on the island.”

Stirling went over to Conway, who was staring

transfixed at the remains of the bridge. He grabbed him roughly by the lapels of his suit and swung the man round to face him.

"You got us all here," he yelled. "Now you have blown up the bridge to keep us here. What the hell is it all about?"

Conway was sweating. He hung limply from Stirling's grasp.

"I've no idea what's going on," he croaked. "It's all a mystery to me."

"Come off it," said Stirling. "You arranged all this and now you've blown up the bloody bridge. What's your game?"

"I didn't arrange all this. I'm not Conway. I'm an actor who was engaged to play the part of Conway. I'm as in the dark as the rest of you."

"That doesn't strike me as a likely story," Allan Preston came in.

"If you let me go," said Conway, "I can show you what I have in my wallet, my driving licence and my Equity card."

Stirling reluctantly let go of Conway, who frantically fished out his wallet and extracted from it his driving licence and Equity card. Both had been issued in the name of Gabriel Marsden.

"Looks like he's telling the truth," observed MacIntyre.

"So what did Conway tell you when he engaged you?" asked Stirling.

"I never met him. It was all done through my agent. And he hadn't met Conway either. It was all done over the phone."

"So what instructions were you given?" enquired Alice Jardine.

"To act as host until Conway himself appeared on the second day. It was supposed to be some elaborate joke that Conway wished to play on the rest of you."

"Didn't you find it all a trifle unbelievable?" asked Cynthia Howard.

"I didn't," confessed Marsden. "It isn't by any means the oddest role I have been asked to play. When you are an actor who hasn't hit the big time, you take what is going and that is often the peculiar stuff that oddballs want done."

"I thought you looked familiar when I first met you," said MacIntyre thoughtfully. "I think that I once saw you in an Ibsen play in a theatre in Islington."

“That's absolutely right. I had a small part in *The Master Builder* there once.”

“You men seem intent on talking the thing to death,” said Cynthia. “What we want is some action. We need to phone the local police and tell them of our predicament.”

Watters coughed discreetly.

“That, unfortunately, will not be possible,” he said. “I had found, just before the explosion, that the telephone was not working and had just ascertained that the line into the island had been cut where it comes into the house.”

“So I will ring them on my mobile.”

“That will also not be possible. There is no mobile signal here on the island. There is no transmitter in the area.”

“Is there a boat on the island?”

“I am afraid not. And no boat can get in or out of the island at the moment. The bay has frozen over and is a sheet of ice.”

“So are you telling us that we are trapped on this island at the mercy of this Conway person?” asked Alice with more than a hint of panic in her voice.

“It would appear so.”

"What the hell does he want?"

"We may be able to find that out," said Marsden. "I was given a disc to be played if it appeared that I needed further instructions. Now seems to be that time."

"Then let's get it and play it," advised Preston.

They all trooped into the house where Marsden unearthed a disc from his room and they went to the sitting room where a player was set up. He inserted the disc and stated it spinning. A cultured voice began to speak.

"Since you are playing this disc, you will have discovered that I was being a little economical with the truth in the message that I sent to you via Marsden. You are not friends of my son. You all contributed, in one way or another, to his desperate end by bullying and abusing him. So I have not invited you to this island to get to know you, but to punish you for what you did to my son. You are trapped on the island and will pay for your misdeeds. The first of you has already paid for her sins. The person you know as Mary bullied my son when they went to the local primary school together and she thus started the process that finished in his committing suicide. She will bully no-one any longer."

The message finished and there was a horrified silence. It was Stirling who reacted first.

"Where the hell is Mary?" he asked.

"I said that I would deal with the breakfast," said Watters. "I told her to have a lie in."

"And where is her room?"

"All the servants' quarters are situated on the attic floor."

"Then we had better get up there and see what has happened to her."

They were quickly up the two flights of stairs but the pace slowed as they entered the corridor that housed Mary's room, all afraid of what they might find there. Watters opened the door carefully and they all craned to see what the room held. A pyjama-clad Mary lay on the bed with the covers thrown back from her body. She had been hit on the head as she slept and, while she lay unconscious, a cushion had been held over her face until she was dead.

They all stood petrified, unable to move. It was MacIntyre who moved and leaned over the body.

"I would say that she has been dead for less than an hour."

"So Conway killed her and then went and blew up the bridge," said a somewhat hysterical Alice.

"No-one went down to the bridge to blow it up," Preston pointed out. "There are no footprints in the snow around the house. No-one has left the house since Mary was killed."

"Maybe they used skis or something."

"Anything that was used to get from the house to the bridge would have left some marks in the snow. The snow has not been disturbed in any way since it fell."

"So how did he manage to blow the bridge up?" asked Cynthia.

"He set it all up before we arrived and used a timer to make sure it went off at the right time this morning," Stirling informed her.

"And, if no-one left the house after Mary was killed," MacIntyre pointed out, "he is still here."

"So let's go and find the bastard," said Stirling. "Cynthia and Alice should stand outside at the north-east and the south-west corners of the house, so that they can, between them, see both front and back doors and all the windows on the ground floor. If Conway comes out of any of these, they should yell blue murder and we'll be after him like a flash. In the meantime, the rest of us will be going over the house with a tooth-comb."

They started in the attic floor. Marsden and Watters were posted at the head of the stairs to stop Conway if he made a bolt for it while the other three went from room to room, making sure that the man was not concealed in any of them and that none of them contained a bolt hole where Conway could hide. When they were satisfied that the attic floor was clear, they descended to the first floor and did the same there. When they were again unable to flush Conway, they repeated the process on the ground floor and then in the cellar, which proved to contain nothing but a fair collection of bottles of wine. They returned to the ground floor and called the two women back inside.

"Didn't you find him?" Cynthia asked.

"He is definitely not in the house," MacIntyre told her.

"But he has to be. He'd have left a trail if he went out in the snow."

"We have to face the truth," said Stirling sternly. "Conway, or the person posing as him, who is also the person who killed Mary, is one of us."

There was a pregnant silence. It was Preston who broke it.

“Has anyone ever met the older Conway?”

There was a general shaking of heads. No-one was admitting that he had ever come across the person who had trapped them all on the island.

“The only two old enough to be young Conway's father are Marsden or Watters,” Preston pointed out.

“Hold on,” said Marsden quickly. “We only have his word that the person seeking revenge is the father. It might well be a brother or a sister. You can't believe anything he says.”

“He's right. We can't jump to conclusions.”

“So what the hell do we do?” asked Alice. “We can't just sit here and let whoever it is do what he pleases.”

“There is something that we can do,” suggested Stirling. “We are all supposed to have contributed to the demise of young Conway. But clearly the person now seeking revenge didn't do any such thing. So let us all admit what it was we did to him. Then we may spot which of the stories is a phoney.”

“It sounds worth doing,” said Cynthia.

“So let me make a start,” said Stirling. “I met

Conway at University. He was a pathetic figure, eager to be liked by all of us. So we took advantage of him. We introduced him to drink and drugs and he never looked back. I have to admit that what I did to him then would definitely have helped him along the path to his eventual suicide."

There was an awkward silence before Alice took up the story.

"I was the headmistress of the primary school to which both Conway and Mary went," she admitted, "although I have to say that I didn't recognise Mary when she served us dinner last night. Conway was a little prig, a most objectionable boy. His father was a big bug in the area and young Conway let you know that he was one of the chosen. I knew that he was being bullied but I thought he deserved it and I did nothing to stop it. The father eventually found out about the bullying and removed his son from the school. And I received a letter from him, saying that he was going to report me to the Teaching Council. That was something that definitely did not help my subsequent career."

It was Marsden who broke the silence that followed.

"If you are an actor, you need to have a second profession to allow you to earn money on the many occasions when there are no acting jobs available. I acted as tutor to young lads who, for one reason or another, were not happy at a school and were eventually educated at home. I lied to you a minute ago. I have met Conway's father. I acted as tutor to his son after he was withdrawn from the local primary school. And he is not here in this house, I can assure you."

"So what did you do to make the young lad continue on the slippery path to suicide?" asked Preston.

Marsden coughed discreetly.

"I am a homosexual. I found the boy attractive. And he was getting for the first time in his life some affection from an adult. He blossomed under my care."

"So that's how you try to justify the awful things that you did to an innocent boy?" said MacIntyre in disgust.

"I don't try to justify it," said Marsden simply. "It was inevitable. It just happened and was wonderful while it lasted."

"No doubt you were twigged eventually," suggested Alice.

"Conway was livid when he found out what had been going on. But he didn't want his son's name dragged through a criminal court. So he sacked me and told me never to darken his door again, while making my employers aware of my sexual proclivities. That was my second occupation gone for ever."

"Our hearts bleed for you," was the comment of Preston.

"And why did you take the job here acting as Conway?" asked Alice.

"When my agent told me about it, I didn't know what to do. But I haven't had work for a while and was desperate. Indeed, I thought it might be interesting to see Conway's reaction when he found out that the person impersonating him was sómeone who had corrupted his son."

There was a bit of a pause before Watters came in hesitantly.

"Young Conway was sent to a public boarding school after that episode," he said. "I looked after the catering at that establishment. The place was run on a shoestring and there was never enough food for the energetic lads. Conway begged me for extra stuff to eat. I granted that to him, but at a price. He was already well versed in sexual acts and was quite happy to accommodate me. That continued as long as I was there."

"And how did you finish up here with the rest of us?" enquired MacIntyre.

"I got sacked from my last catering job," Watters admitted," for inappropriate behaviour with a minor. When I got offered a job as butler here, I jumped at the chance. I might have known that it was too good to be true."

There was a short silence before Preston took over the story.

"I was at the school that Watters just talked about," he said, "although I had no idea that Watters was indulging in inappropriate practices. I wasn't interested in that sort of thing. But what I was interested in was money since my parents were not all that wealthy and kept me short of pocket money. So I used to beat up Conway unless he paid me not to. I guess he had a pretty bad time, one way and another, at that awful school."

There was a long silence when Preston had

finished.

"I guess that we were a pretty bad bunch to poor old Conway," said Stirling at length. He turned to Cynthia and MacIntyre. "I wonder what the other two of you did to the poor little bugger."

"It is no great mystery in my case," said Cynthia. "I was having an affair with a friend of Conway's while he was up at university. I was passionate about the friend, but he wasn't all that interested in me. So I thought that I would get him jealous by having a passionate affair with Conway. It worked all right. The friend came racing back to me, so I dropped Conway like a hot potato. He had doted on me and thought that he had found love at last. When I ditched him, he took it very hard. He went into a decline. I've never seen anything like it. I'm surprised that he didn't commit suicide at that point in his life."

"It was at that time when he was highly depressed that I came across him," said MacIntyre. "I befriended him and helped him get back his confidence. But I have to admit that I didn't do all that out of the goodness of my heart. I was in a bad financial hole at the time with the prospect of going to prison for fraud staring me in the face if I couldn't get a hold of a considerable quantity of money. That money I managed to prise out of Conway, so my bacon was saved. But, when Conway realised that I had only been using him, he went into an even deeper depression. And it was not long after that that he committed suicide."

They sat thinking about what they had heard. None of them had come out of the confessions with flying colours.

"So, is one of these revelations obviously phoney?" asked Cynthia.

"They all sounded very believable," admitted Stirling ruefully. "But I suppose that anyone who wanted to slip in among us would make sure that he had a story about his involvement with Conway that that was eminently plausible."

The silence that followed was broken by Alice.

"After these confessions, I am wondering why some of us accepted the invitation to come here. Three of us needed the work. As for me, Conway ruined my career, so that anythng that I could get from him for free, I was prepared to grab with both hands. But what prompted the rest of you to come here?"

"I am not doing too well these days," Preston

admitted ruefully "If you are livng a bit hand to mouth, you don't pass up the chance of a few days good living."

"I guess that goes for me as well," said MacInytre. "A few days' eating and drinking well has its attractions when you are on the bread line."

They all looked at Stirling.

"I was suspicious of the invitation from the start," he admitted. "But life has been a bit dull recently. And I do like a bit of adventure. I thought that it might liven things up to come here. I didn't really bargain on my life being in danger."

All eyes had turned to Cynthia.

"I seem to be the only one of you," she said defiantly, "who has had attacks of conscience about what we did to young Conway. It has troubed me ever since. When I got the invitation to come here, I felt that I had to come to see if I could do something for the father whose son I had treated so dreadfully in the past."

The others looked a trifle ashamed that they had not felt the same same about what they had done to Conway in the past. It was to hide his embarrassment that Preston turned to Stirling.

“Have you any other thoughts about what we should be doing?”

“I have. If the police come here eventually and find all of us murdered, they might be somewhat baffled as to what has happened. If they find only one person still alive, I want them to be damned sure they know that he has murdered the rest of us. So I propose to keep a diary each day of everything that is happening. I hope you will all sign each day's story to show that it is not just some idiot's drivelling. Indeed, why don't you all keep diaries as well.”

“I am sure that we would all be happy to sign your accounts of the day's events. But, if somebody is intent on killing us all, won't he take all your jottings and burn them?” asked MacIntyre.

“I noticed yesterday that there was a photocopier on the premises. I was intending to make lots of photocopies of the diary entries and hide them all over the place,” said Stirling. “He wouldn't surely be able to find all of them.”

“Sounds a good idea,” said Alice. “Any more brilliant ideas?”

“During daylight hours, we should all try to keep in the sight of other people. At night, things will be more difficult. You should try to keep in groups of three for safety. And, when you go up to bed, you should lock your door and leave the key in the lock. The bastard may have a skeleton key that fits all the doors."

They all seemed happy to have been given instructions as to how they should behave in the future.

"What about Mary?" said Preston suddenly. "We can't just leave her to rot away in her bed."

"We should preserve, as best we can, her body and any others that we may later have," suggested MacIntyre, "so that the police can find out what they can about her death. There was a bit of a dip running along the side of the lawn. It will now be filled with snow. We should bury the body in there. That should give some chance of preserving it for some considerable time."

And that was what they did. MacIntyre and Watters, watched by the others, carried the body down and buried it deep in the snow beside the lawn. Everyone was looking a trifle depressed when they made their way back into the house.

CHAPTER 2

Watters went off to try to rustle up something for lunch. The others mooned around the house, uncertain as to the best way to fill the time. Alice sidled up to Stirling.

"You are certainly the man of action," she said admiringly. "While the rest of us were panicking and wondering what to do, you were in there like a flash, making order out of the chaos and forcing us all to be be rational."

"I have always reacted well," he said modestly, "to new situations."

"In fact you were displaying all the characteristics of the kind of man who has arranged to have us marooned here."

He looked at her a trifle askance.

"You think that I am the one who has arranged all this?"

"It seems quite a possibility."

"So why aren't you denouncing me to the others?"

She smiled archly at him.

"I thought that we might come to a private agreement."

“What sort of agreement?”

“That you might let me leave the island with you. You must have made some arrangement as to how to get off the island once you have finished your work here.”

“And why would I be inclined to let you leave unharmed?”

“Because I could make your stay on the island even more wonderful than you had expected. I am pretty good at making a man think he's in heaven when he is in bed with me.”

Stirling burst out laughing.

“You really are naïve,” he stated. “If I were the man behind all this, I would accept your offer and then strangle you before I left the island. Why would you expect a murderer to keep his word? But I will do you the favour of not reporting what you have just proposed to the others. I don't think they would be too happy at your trying to make a pact at their expense with the killer.”

It was some time later that MacIntyre was walking through the drawing room where he found Stirling in a chair reading a book that he had taken from the bookshelves. He sat down beside him and engaged him in small talk. In the middle of the conversation, he looked at his watch.

“Shouldn't Watters have announced lunch by now?” he asked. “It's getting quite late.”

A fearful thought settled in both of their minds. They looked at one another in horror, got up and ran out of the drawing room and made for the kitchen. As they entered that room, they both came to an abrupt halt. Watters lay beside the table that occupied the centre of the room. Like Mary, he had been struck on the head and the cushion that had then been used to smother him lay by his side. MacIntyre knelt beside the body to confirm that the man was dead, but neither of them had doubted for a moment that he was beyond help.

“He is more ruthless than I thought,” said Stirling. “I guess we will have to be more careful about not being on our own in future.”

“Why do you say 'he'?” asked MacIntyre. “Killing in this way can be done as easily by a woman as by a man.”

They notified the others of the latest occurrence and then Watters was solemnly carried outside and carefully interred in the snow beside the earlier victim.

When they had all returned to the drawing room and were sitting around silently, still in shock, Stirling spoke to them.

"Our company is now reduced to six and we should be in no doubt what is the fate that awaits each and every one of us if we lose vigilance for a moment."

"But what the hell can we do to stop him picking us off one by one?" demanded Alice.

"We must never be on our own. Then we would be too easy to pick off. And we shouldn't go around in pairs. The other half of our pair might be the killer. We must keep together in threes. I would suggest, for the moment, that we should have one trio of Cynthia, Marsden and me to be together at all times and another of MacIntyre, Alice and Preston."

"And who is going to prepare the meals?" asked Marsden plaintively. "That's women's work."

"We'll have none of that sexist attitude here," said Cynthia firmly. "You will help with the meals or you won't eat. We'll set up a rota and each trio will prepare a meal in its turn."

And so it was arranged. Nothing else of interest happened until they all trooped up the stairs together to go to bed. They had all gone into their rooms when MacIntyre let out a loud shriek. They all raced out again onto the landing to find out what was amiss with him.

"The bastard has been up and stolen my key," he yelled. "I can't lock myself in."

The others went back into their rooms to check. They all came out to report that the same thing had happened to them. That is, all of them except Marsden.

"I had the good sense to lock my room up and take the key away with me," he said smugly.

The others were inclined to look at him with suspicion in their eyes.

"But what do we do," wailed Alice, "to keep ourselves safe with no key to lock up the room?"

"Wedge a chair under the door handle," said Preston. "He would have to make a lot of noise forcing the door open. That would give you enough time to yell for help and arm yourself with a weapon with which to defend yourself."

They all slept a little uneasily that night but were all still present and unharmed in the morning. It was not until later that evening that any incident occurred.

The trio that included Howard were preparing the dinner when Cynthia realised that Marsden was not with the other two. She turned to where Stirling was preparing vegetables.

"I sent Marsden to the larder to get some stuff. He hasn't returned."

They looked askance at one another and then ran from the room. They came to a stop at the entrance to the larder. Marsden lay dead on the floor. He, like the others, had been hit on the head and then smothered with a cushion. There was no doubt that he was dead.

They found the other three in the sitting room, reading. They told them what had happened. There was a horrified silence.

"Did any of you leave this room at any time?" Cynthia broke the silence.

"Each of the men went to the toilet at some point," Alice answered.

"Were they long enough away to have got to the kitchen and killed Marsden?"

"Hold on just a minute," MacIntyre came in. "You and Stirling were down there with Marsden in the kitchen. You could more easily than either of us have slipped out and let Marsden have it. Could either of you swear that the other was in his sight at all times recently?"

"I guess not."

"So we all could have done it with the exception of Alice. She seems to have had someone else with her at all times."

It was an uncomfortable meal that evening, not that any of them had much of an appetite. And they all looked at each other with grave suspicion as they parted in the corridor outside the bedrooms. The sleep was even more fitful than it had been on the previous nights.

With only five of them still left alive, they tended to congregate together, not willing to be in a position to be added to the list of the departed. But meals had to be prepared and visits to the toilet had to be made. So there were occasions when people were vulnerable to attack. But they had got through most of the next day without incident and were all together in the sitting room just after dinner when there was suddenly an explosion from some distance away in the house.

After a moment of shock while they tried to come

to terms with what was happening, they panicked and ran from the room and down the stairs, searching for the source of the explosion. In the cellar, they found that some sort of explosive device had been detonated in a container in one of the bays. It had done little damage, the purpose of the explosion to produce a lot of noise and create panic.

"What do you think that was all in aid of?" asked MacIntyre.

"He is trying to get us all scared so that we will be easier to deal with," suggested Stirling.

"So he's doing a grand job," said Alice. "I am shaking like a leaf."

"Where the hell is Preston?" asked Cynthia in a frightened voice. "He's not here."

They found his dead body in one of the toilets. He had been smothered like the others. They trooped back, very subdued, into the sitting room.

"One of us did this," said Stirling. "Can we work out which one? We all panicked when we heard the explosion and ran out without thinking or giving much thought to what anyone else was doing. Does anyone remember what Preston did?"

But no-one could remember. They had all been

too much concerned to find out where the explosion had been and whether they were liable to be blown up in a further explosion or burned alive if the blast had started a fire. And no-one was very clear as to where the others had been as they rushed around.

“So that's what the explosion was all about,” observed MacIntyre. “He gets us all in such a panic that we all rushed around, so concerned with our own safety that we don't pay any attention to what others are doing. And, while we are all rushing around like scalded cats, he clobbers Preston, drags him into the toilet and kills him.”

“So one of us is still intent on getting rid of all the rest of us,” said a white-faced Alice in a very small, frightened voice.

“Did you ever doubt it?” asked Cynthia contemptuously. “Did you expect him to have a sudden change of heart?”

“One can hope.”

“Then give up hope. Unless we can work out who the bastard is and nobble him before he gets us all, I wouldn't give much for our chances.”

“So let's try to work out who he is,” suggested Stirling.

But with no clues as to whom the killer might be, the discussion did not last long. They carried out the body and added it to the graveyard in the snow. And all of them seemed relieved when they could split up and go to bed.

The next day, they tended to huddle together, looking sideways at one another. They were preparing a meal in the kitchen when Alice suddenly collapsed to the floor. Cynthia went to her to try to help and also collapsed. It was immediately thereafter that the other two collapsed as well. MacIntyre was the first to resurface and went round trying to revive the others. He was unsuccessful when it came to Alice She had been strangled.

When the body had been taken out and buried in the snow, the remaining trio went back to the sitting room and regarded each other glumly.

"What caused us all to collapse one after the other?" asked Cynthia.

"There was a gas cylinder at the south end of the kitchen which had been opened a small fraction," replied MacIntyre. "When the gas got to us and we inhaled it, we collapsed."

"Who went to the south end of the kitchen just

before we collapsed?" asked Cynthia.

"I guess we all did at one time or another," said Stirling. "And we have no idea how long it would take for the gas concentration to be enough to knock us all out. So it could have been any one of us."

He paused as a thought struck him

"But we know who it was who surfaced first. MacIntyre could easily have strangled Alice before he aroused us two."

"Hold on," shouted MacIntyre, as the pair looked menacingly at him. "It would have been easy enough for one of you two to have kept well away from the gas until everyone else was out, killed Alice and then faked still being under the influence of the gas until I came to revive you."

"I guess that could be true," said Cynthia reluctantly.

They watched each other nervously during the rest of the day and all appeared happy to get to bed where they could relax.

The next morning, MacIntyre was first to emerge from his bedroom. He shouted to the others that he was about to go downstairs. Cynthia came out of her bedroom and they waited for Stirling to join them.

When he appeared, they started down the stairs. It was not until they had reached the kitchen that the other two realised that Stirling was not with them.

They looked at each other, not quite sure what to do, and stood irresolute for some little time. It was then that Stirling rushed into the room and confronted MacIntyre.

"You've been leading us up the garden path," he yelled. "I have just had a good look round your room. You're a doctor. What's your real connection with Conway? Did you diagnose that he was depressed when he had something a lot worse wrong with him? Is that why he committed suicide? Because he had found out that he was suffering some fatal disease, not because he was bullied?"

"You've got it all wrong," pleaded MacIntyre. But, before he could say any more, a furious Stirling had hit him a savage punch which knocked him backward. He stumbled, fell and hit his head a sickening blow on the corner of the oven. His body sank down to the floor with blood oozing from the nasty wound in the back of his head.

Stirling stared stupidly at the body, shocked at what he had done.

"You got it all wrong," said Cynthia. "I knew he was a doctor. But he wasn't a medical doctor. He was a doctor of philosophy."

Stirling looked up at her. She was standing a little away from him and she had a gun in her hand that was pointed at his head.

"What the hell is this?" he asked.

"There are only two of us left on the island," she said, "so it becomes pretty obvious who has been responsible for all the killing, doesn't it? I found this gun hidden in your room when I searched it yesterday. Now I wonder why anyone would bring with him a gun when he was about to enjoy a few day's hospitality at another's expense."

CHAPTER 3

Detective Chief Inspector Ian Forsyth was the most successful detective that the Lothian and Borders Police Force ever had. He was a genius at logical deduction and could spot anomalies in a reasoned argument that everyone else had missed. He solved a number of high profile cases that had had the rest of us baffled.

I, Alastair MacRae, had been his sergeant during most of the time that he was at the peak of his success. He was not the easiest man to work for. Indeed, the first murder case in which I worked with him was so traumatic that I feared for a while that my career in the police would be finished forever. You will find the details in a story that I have entitled *The Crime Committee.* But it turned out all right in the end and we became an established team.

But that first case established the relationship between us. When you have seen Forsyth at his worst, as well as his best, ignoring every rule in the book as to how to conduct an investigation, you are a little short on the hero worship. And, to give Forsyth his due, he is not much into the belief that the boss and the hired help are different species. So we got on together as a team and I had the impression that he regarded me affectionately as a rather dim version of the son that he had never had.

When he retired, I carried on for a bit with his successor. But the magic had gone out of investigations and I eventually retired early and devoted my time to golf and writing up accounts of his more celebrated cases.

We stayed in touch. We had a drink or lunch from time to time in one of the hostelries that we had frequented while still working, and I was invited occasionally to dinner at his house.

He had been married at one time but the union had ended in an acrimonious divorce. He is now looked after by a housekeeper who is a first rate cook, so I always looked forward to these meals, which were accompanied by a sufficiency of excellent wine and finished off with malt whisky accompanying the coffee.

So I was a trifle surprised when he rang up one morning and asked if he could come round to see me at my house in Liberton. I was only too happy to agree and he turned up shortly thereafter in a taxi, bearing a large file. He is not very keen on driving and, although he owns a large, flashy car, he does a lot of travelling by taxi.

He refused my offer of a whisky, saying that it was a little early in the day for him to indulge, so we settled for coffees and, once I had sat us down with mugs of the brew, he revealed why he was there.

"The Lothian and Borders Police has been struggling to solve a case that has erupted on their doorstep. The Chief Super is convinced that he holds the solution to the mystery but the Chief Constable has this nagging feeling that all is not as simple as it would appear. I meet him from time to time at the Golf Club and he has asked me to have a look at the case and give him my opinion."

"They just can't do without you," I suggested.

He inclined his head in acknowledgement of the compliment and continued.

"I only agreed to accept the commission if they also added you to my team. I hope that you will agree to serve. There will be a small honorarium for you at the end."

"You need a leg man to do all the hard grind," I stated.

"That is not my expertise," he pointed out. "My

talents lie in a different direction. But that very much is what you are good at. Each to his own speciality. That is what made us a good team."

"I would be happy to join you in any enterprise that you think is worth pursuing. What is the case all about?"

"A group of eight people were lured to an island off the east coast and marooned there after the heavy snow storm in January. They had all been involved in one way or another with the denigration of a young man who had subsequently committed suicide. He was the son of a landowner and financial tycoon, called Conway. It became apparent that they were there to be punished for their parts in the young man's demise and they were gradually killed one by one."

"Rather like that Agatha Christie story entitled Ten Little," I paused, "Black Gentlemen."

"Changed to Ten Little Indians later," he pointed out, "so as not to give offence. It is true that in that story a number of people lured to an island all perished. But there the resemblance ends. In the Christie story, the villain had persuaded the doctor in the group to certify him as dead even although he was very much still alive, thus allowing him freedom to kill the remaining survivors, including the doctor, with ease. No such thing happened here. There was no medical doctor present and all the people who perished were all quite dead."

"How do we know all this if they were all found dead?" I asked.

"Several of them left accounts of what was happening."

"I am surprised," I said, "that the killer did not remove all these accounts to deepen the mystery of what had happened."

"The victims had thought that that might happen," he told me, "and had made photocopies of their jottings and hidden them all over the place. But such foresight was not necessary. Something appeared to have gone wrong with the original plan."

"The best laid schemes of mice and men," I quoted.

"Exactly. The accounts stopped after only three of them were left alive. When the final two found the third last survivor dead, it must have been obvious to the innocent one of the pair that the other one was the killer."

"So who were the last two?"

"A man called Stirling and a woman called Howard."

"And which of these two had killed all the others?" I asked.

"That is not entirely clear," he admitted. "It might have been either of them. You see, she had apparently shot him dead. But he had already managed to slip poison into her food or drink. So both of them were found dead. You can take your pick as to who was the guilty person and who was the innocent one."

"And who was it who actually owned the island?" I asked.

"It was owned by Conway. The young Conway had always enjoyed his time there. But, after he died, his father turned against it and it had not been used for some time."

"And were the police not a trifle suspicious of Conway?"

"They were. But he had not been near the island and, however much one might believe that he had instigated the crimes, there was no evidence that could link him to the happenings on the island

"So what is it that you want me to do?" I

enquired.

He handed over the file that he had been nursing all this while.

"I would like you to read this file so that you are fully acquainted with all that is known about the case. I will return later this afternoon and we will then discuss how we are to proceed."

I studied the file after he had left and, by the time that he returned in the afternoon, I was fully conversant with all that the file contained. This time, when I offered him refreshment, he was happy to accept my offer of a Glenlivet malt whisky. I poured us each generous measures and added a little spring water to each. When we had both sampled the golden liquid, I asked what he wanted done.

"The house on the island had not been in use for some time before the events occurred in which we are interested," he explained. "So all the food and drink that was consumed over the fateful period had all to be brought from somewhere. I want you to find out from whom it was purchased and obtain from that organisation a complete list of all that was sent to the house."

I could see no reason why he should wish this

information. But this had been true often in the past and there had always proved eventually to be good reason for his wanting apparently irrelevant information.

“That shouldn't prove difficult,” I said. “Is there anything else that you want done?”

“I want you to find out whether either of Stirling or Howard are related to Conway, the father of the boy who committed suicide, and also determine who would run the Conway estate if he was sent to prison for being behind the murders on the island. And, since a man of his standing would not survive long in prison, you should find out who would inherit everything on his demise.”

“It will be attended to.”

“You will have noticed that the police found evidence that a hovercraft had landed on the beach close to the jetty in the bay. Have you any observations about when that was likely to have occurred?” he asked.

“A hovercraft makes a lot of noise. If it had appeared on the island while the occupants were still making notes of events, such an occurrence would have been reported,” I suggested. “It seems more likely that the killer had arranged to be picked up by the hovercraft once he, or she, had completed the mission on the island. The rescuer would have been a bit nonplussed to find his boss dead also and would have shot off into the great unknown before the events on the island were discovered."

"It does seem the most likely explanation," he agreed.

We had another Glenlivet and talked of other things before he departed.

It took me two days to find out all the things that he wanted to know. When I got back home on the second day, I rang him. He suggested that I visit him at his home by taxi and this I did. When I had been sat down in his sitting room with a large Glenlivet by my side, I reported on what I had discovered.

"I found out which supplier had provided all the food and drink for the island. He was rung up, allegedly by a Mr Conway, and was paid by a cash draft which arrived in the post a few days before the stuff was delivered to the island."

I handed over a list of all that had been sent to the island. He gave it a cursory glance and then laid it beside him.

“And, as to the other matter?” he asked.

“Howard and Stirling are the children of two of Conway's sisters, now deceased. He has the power of attorney to manage the estate should anything render Conway unable to do so. Should Conway die, the pair are the principal beneficiaries under his will.”

“And, now that these two are dead, who will inherit in the event of Conway's death?”

“A more distant relative called Jane Goodwin. She was a bit of a tearaway as a child, needing a good lawyer to keep her out of prison after a number of very unpleasant episodes. But she has now settled down, has married an ex-SAS man called Bernard Watkins and lives in Galashiels.”

He sat thinking about the information that I had supplied. I took a sip of my Glenlivet.

“I also enquired whether a hovercraft had been hired by anyone at the relevant time. One was, allegedly by a club to do some botanical work around the islands. But the club appears not to exist and the money paid for the hire was from an account which had only just been opened and has, since that time, been discontinued.

“Interesting,” he said, still brooding.

I thought that it was time for me to ask the all important question.

“Have you solved the mystery as to what the events on the island were all about?”

He thought carefully before replying. He is always cautious about what information he is willing to divulge during an investigation. He is intent on maintaining his reputation for infallibility. So not too much indication of his thinking must be given early on in case things don't turn out as expected. And, if they are correct, he still does not wish any premature indication of the solution to be given that might detract from the impact that the final revelation is intended to produce.

“I believe,” he said eventually, “that I know who was responsible for the events that took place on the island. But the Chief Constable will not be too convinced by logical arguments since such thinking is not his strong point.”

“No,” I agreed. “He likes to look at fingerprints and bloodstains. Do you think that you can provide him with the sort of proof that will have him watering at the mouth?”

“I am convinced that I will be able to do so,” he

said somewhat smugly.

CHAPTER 4

It was two days later that I was invited by Forsyth to dinner at his house. He suggested that I come by taxi and he also suggested that it might be best to bring pyjamas, a razor and a toothbrush so that I could stay with him overnight and therefore be able to enjoy as much wine and whisky as I pleased without worrying about how to get home safely. When I arrived, I discovered that I was the only guest that night.

Nothing was said about the case during the pre-dinner drinks nor during the course of the meal. We discussed everything but that. It was not until we were back in his sitting room with cups of coffee and glasses of Glenlivet by our sides that he brought up the subject of the doings on the island.

“Having seen all the evidence that was available to the police,” he asked, “have you formed an opinion as to who was responsible for the events on the island?”

“I would plump for Stirling.” I replied. “He made sure that things done on the island were performed in the way that he wanted.”

“But he was apparently shot by Miss Howard,” Forsyth pointed out.

“I verified that Stirling was the only one who was licensed to own a firearm. So I assume that he took that with him to the island in case it might be needed. But Howard had been suspicious of him for some time, had stolen the gun from wherever he had hidden it and used it when the third-last person was found dead and it was obvious that her suspicions had been correct. Unfortunately for her, he had already managed to put poison into something that she had eaten or drunk.”

“And what is your view as to whether it was Conway senior who had persuaded Stirling to carry out his revenge for him or whether Stirling was acting on his own behalf?”

“I can't see Stirling being worried enough about young Conway's demise to want to take revenge. It put him in the position of being one of Conway's heirs, after all. I imagine Conway persuaded him to do the killings for him. Perhaps he threatened to change his will unless Stirling toed the line and did what he was told. But I doubt that you will ever be able to prove Conway's involvement.”

“Your solution and your assessment of Conway's involvement agrees totally with the one that the Chief

Super has put forward as the correct one," Forsyth told me.

There was something in the tone of his voice that made me look at him suspiciously.

"But it is not the solution at which you have arrived," I hazarded.

"It is not."

"So what is your solution?"

He thought carefully as to how he should lead me to the final explanation.

"Did it never occur to you that it was very stupid of the killer to reveal his real name to the others. Some of the notes made by the victims would almost certainly have survived a search by the killer and the police would then be well aware of who had caused all the mayhem even although he had escaped from the island by hovercraft."

"It does seem a bit peculiar now that you mention it," I admitted. "But, of course, Howard knew who he was so he couldn't really fool her."

"I am sure that he could have found some convincing reason to give her for using an assumed name."

"You may well be right," I said uneasily.

"You were surprised," he suggested, "that I required a list of all the food and drink that had been delivered to the island."

"I was," I admitted. "I could see no reason why you would wish it."

"That was because you had not looked carefully enough at the post-mortem reports on some of the victims."

"So enlighten me."

"Two of the victims had consumed some rather exotic food that day that was not on the list that you had acquired."

"The two in question no doubt being Stirling and Howard."

"Exactly."

That astonished me.

"Why would they take food to the island," I asked, "and consume it in secrecy?"

Another thought struck me.

"If she was eating secretly, how did he manage to poison her?"

"There is an alternative explanation," he said, "as to why they had food inside them that was not on the list."

I couldn't think of any such explanation and had to ask him what it was.

"That Howard and Stirling were the two people who arrived that final day on the hovercraft."

I was now totally confused. Forsyth could see that and took pity on me.

"Let me run a possible scenario past you," he said. "It might help you to more easily understand what really went on. Let us suppose that Stirling and Howard, who are Conway's heirs, decided that they wanted to get control of the Conway estate early. They thought up this scheme for staging on the island a seeking of revenge by Conway for what had happened to his son. But they needed two of the participants to actually be the people who would carry out the murders. With two people involved, it would be easier to confuse and then kill the others. But where could they find two people who would be prepared to kill off the rest of the visitors to the island?"

"Where indeed?"

"What about a near relative," he suggested, "who was a bit of a tearaway in her youth, and had committed several acts which would have landed her in prison had her parents not obtained the services of a first class lawyer, and her husband, who had been in the SAS and had no doubt been involved in some hairy actions in his time."

"If they were offered a large chunk of the monies that Stirling and Howard would eventually inherit," I said thoughtfully, "they might well have accepted. In fact, they would probably have jumped at the chance to make what they would regard as some easy money. They were leading a pretty meagre existence in Galashiels."

"And, while apparently going along with the scheme that the other two had come up with," he suggested, "they might also have seen this as an opportunity to get the whole of the estate for themselves."

"Goodwin being the next in line, if the other two died," I said excitedly. "And Howard and Stirling were unlikely to suspect that the other two would be able to doublecross them."

"The original plan," Forsyth continued, "would be for Goodwin and Watkins to go to the island under fake names but with a convincing story of their involvement with the young Conway, to gradually kill off the others on the island and then be taken off by the other two by hovercaraft after leaving some convincing proof there that Conway had been behind the scheme."

"Do you believe that Stirling and Howard intended to take them off," I asked, "and not to kill them and leave them there?"

"We will never be sure," he suggested. "But I would give them the benefit of the doubt and assume that they intended to play fair."

"But Goodwin and Watkins didn't intend to play fair," I pointed out.

"No. They registered on the island as Stirling and Howard and, when the hovercraft arrived to take them off, they found some excuse to take the newcomers up to the house where they shot one and poisoned the other before making their escape."

"And you think that everything that they did while they were on the island was always strictly in character with the roles that they were playing?"

"I imagine," said Forsyth, "that they would be worried that Stirling and Howard had planted bugs on the island and that were recording everything that went on. So they would be careful not to depart from their pretended roles all the time that they were on the island."

I thought about his explanation of the happenings on the island. It all fitted and explained all the anomalies. I had no doubt that he had arrived at the correct solution. But I had to draw his attention to the fact that it was all theorising.

"A good defence attorney," I said, "will point out to the jury that your ideas are all airy-fairy theorising with no proof."

"But of course there is proof that Goodwin and Watkins were involved," he said. "You should know by now that I would not come out with a logical theory unless I also had proof to back it up that a jury would accept. I asked the Galashiels police to have Goodwin and Watkins taken in on the pretext that the authorities were trying to find out more about Stirling and Howard from the people who had known them. In the course of the interview they were give cups of coffee."

He looked at me enquiringly.

"And once they had gone," I suggested, "the fingerprints from the coffee cups were matched with fingerprints taken from the rooms on the island occupied by the people claiming to be Stirling and

Howard."

"And found to be a match."

"So another triumph is added to the long list under your name."

He tried to look modest with the usual lack of success. He got up and refreshed our whisky glasses. He also handed me a cheque drawn on an account of the Lothian and Borders Police. It was larger than I had anticipated.

"They have been more generous than I remember from the old days," I said.

"I think that the Chief Constable was so pleased to have scored one over the Chief Super, that he was carried away."

"It was a pleasure working with you again," I said. "I would have been happy to do it for nothing. I can only hope that some intractable cases will occur in the Lothian and Borders area in the future and that they will need to call on your services once again."